Heloise
and
Bellinis

To Michael

[signature]

1991-92

Heloise and Bellinis

A NOVEL BY
HARRY CIPRIANI

TRANSLATED FROM THE ITALIAN
BY RONALD STROM

Arcade Publishing · NEW YORK
Little, Brown and Company

First English-language Edition

This is a work of fiction. Names, characters, places,
and incidents are either the product of the author's
imagination or, if real, are used fictitiously.

Library of Congress Cataloging-in-Publication Data

Cipriani, Arrigo.
    [Eloisa e il Bellini. English]
    Heloise and Bellinis : a novel / by Harry Cipriani. — 1st English-
    language ed.
        p.   cm.
    Translation of: Eloisa e il Bellini.
    ISBN 1-55970-144-7
    I. Title.
    PQ4863.I677E413   1991
    853'.914—dc20   91-10681

Published in the United States
by Arcade Publishing, Inc., New York,
a Little, Brown company

10 9 8 7 6 5 4 3 2 1

BP

*Published simultaneously in Canada
by Little, Brown & Company (Canada) Limited*

Printed in the United States of America

To My Faithful Olivetti,
Model ETV300,
For Writing This Tale with
Almost No Help from the Author

Speak Not,
Please,
Not a Word.
Let the Sounds
Of Your Splendid Body
Be the Splash of the Spent Wave
Breaking on a Silent Shore,
The Murmur of the Breeze
Through a Stand of Fir Trees,
The Groan of Riggings
In a Boat,
The Mournful Creaking of the Stays,
The Howling Rage in Every Storm,
The Still Calm
Of a Sun-flayed Desert Vastness.
But Speak Not,
Please,
I Beg You,
Not a Word.

CONTENTS

Heloise
and
Bellinis

Then he said calmly, "Maria, send me the tug."

Her curiosity was aroused, and for a moment she looked at the terribly pale face that had not moved.

Little puffs of steam from his nostrils condensed and froze on the tips of his thick white beard.

She came close and brought her moist lips to his ear. Very softly she whispered, "I can send you the cruiser, my darling, or a destroyer, if you like, but not the tugboat. I can't."

A shiver ran through him, and one by one the icicles slowly broke away from his beard.

Two frozen tears, hard and hopeless, shattered his pupils forever.

THE END

INTRODUCTION

Only the last page of a long novel was found on the beach at Acapulco roughly forty years after the big cracker went off.

Exhaustive research on the man with the beard showed that he was anything but the hero of the book—quite the contrary, he appeared inexplicably only in the last twenty lines. What was established with certainty is that he was born in the year 2001 in Alabama, the son of a Czech mother and an Austro-American father. His family name was Smith, because he had been legitimized by his father, but his given name was never known.

The sad story was set in the port of Barletta and had to do with the unrequited love of a young tugboat for a pretty little pilot boat.

It also turned out that Smith, the man with the beard, was devastated by the thought that there was no way he could change what was a hopeless situation. That very afternoon he practically gulped down three liter-bottles of Château d'Yquem. Totally drunk, he identified with the little pilot boat and, as we just saw, asked Maria, the wife of the doorman at the Göteborg Hilton, to place the tugboat in his hands.

No plausible reason was ever found for Maria to call him "darling." Aside from their fleeting romance of no importance, the only explanation for her use of that term of endearment might be the subsequently discovered fact that at the start of the afternoon there had actually been six bottles of Château d'Yquem, and no trace was ever found of the three bottles that should have been left over after the three that Smith drank.

It also needs saying that by the end of the book, the year 2040, he had gone blind. And, as mentioned, his birthplace and the identity of his parents were the subject of extensive and interesting research.

His parents had met quite by chance in Beirut on July 14 of the year 2000.

His mother, Heloise Svejk, had been a widow for just two days. Her late husband, a guerrilla fighter in the Christian militia, died from the consequences of being kicked by a horse. She did not love him, but two years earlier she had gone with him from Czechoslovakia to Beirut solely to get out from behind the Iron Curtain, which in the late 1990s had come crashing back down in a number of East European countries.

His parents' story began around eleven o'clock on that scorching day in July.

CHAPTER ONE

In which we make the acquaintance of George Smith and the widow Heloise Svejk.

Around eleven o'clock on the morning of Friday, July 14, 2000, Private George Smith was breathlessly chasing a hand grenade along the sidewalk of the Avenue d'Angleterre in Beirut; he had forgotten to pull the pin before he threw it.

At that very moment Mrs. Heloise Svejk was crossing the same street from east to west. She balanced the empty coffin of her husband on her right shoulder. Three of his former comrades, guerrillas of the Christian militia, effortfully helped her. They were on their way back from the common grave in the cemetery. They were returning the coffin to the undertaker, who usually bought back returns at half price.

A platoon of Fusiliers of Christ stopped Mrs. Svejk and her companions and asked to see the papers for the coffin at the very moment that Private Smith, a few steps away, was busy retrieving his unexploded grenade. Things looked very bad for Mrs. Svejk, because

5

she had bought the coffin on the black market without a certificate of purchase. But what was taken for the threatening presence of peace-loving Private Smith sent the fusiliers rushing off, together with the guerrillas. Left alone with her heavy burden, Mrs. Svejk made a strenuous effort to lift the coffin onto her head. George Smith suddenly caught sight of her as she moved slowly down the avenue, quivering from the exertion. George was a private in the peacekeeping armed forces of the United States of America. He had been in Beirut for two years, and it had been two years since he set eyes on a real woman.

It would not be true, however, to say that any woman would have aroused such keen interest in George; the truth is that Mrs. Svejk was altogether special. It is absolutely true that the strain of her exertions made her quiver as she moved slowly down the avenue, but it is just as true that the best possible way of describing Mrs. Svejk would be to say that she was a beautiful woman always all aquiver. So without further ado: Mrs. Svejk was a beautiful woman all aquiver. Just so.

Indeed, the only part of her body that did not quiver as she walked perilously balanced on the high heels of two dusty black evening shoes sheathing two slender feet that supported not-too-thin but perfectly proportioned ankles, was her smooth, streamlined calves. Every other part of her exceptional physique seemed to be set aquiver together—from the stupendous thighs to the hips marked ever so faintly by the outline of her almost invisible panties, hips that suddenly narrowed at the waist, a stem that supported in delicate balance a marvelous quivering bosom that descended in front of two slender, sinuous shoulders, to which was grafted a long neck barely shadowed by a jaw that jutted slightly forward. The lips were somewhat pouty, slashed out under an extremely delicate Greek nose that separated two dark eyes—surprised, wide open, frowning, as clear as they could be, and a bit innocently guilty as well, with the right eye occasionally covered by a stray lock of unkempt ebony hair. Her purple silk dress, scarcely more than a rag torn in hundreds of places, allowed a glimpse of small areas of wonderfully healthy olive-toned breast, stomach, and marvelously smooth thighs.

END OF CHAPTER ONE

CHAPTER TWO

The actual meeting of George and Heloise.

So it is no surprise that George Smith was totally over-whelmed by sudden desire the moment he saw Mrs. Svejk. He quickly slipped the grenade into one of his socks, along with a pack of Lucky Strikes, and asked: "Pardon me, can I be of any help?"

Mrs. Svejk's tone was resigned, as if she had seen everything and accepted everything: "If you like."

George was a good giant. The pointed face he had inherited from his Austro-Hungarian father seemed always on the verge of an ironic smile. His blond hair and blue eyes came from an American mother of Swed-ish descent.

George was so overcome by emotion that he stood motionless for a long time without uttering a word. He walked alongside Mrs. Svejk in the burning sun, and his sweat seemed to be the only source of coolness. After walking side by side for an hour, they reached the undertaker's premises. George said: "Let me handle it."

The undertaker was standing in the doorway of a shed full of coffins. "Want to sell it?" he asked.

"Yes."

"How much do you want?"

"Seventy dollars."

"I'll give you fifty."

"First I'll break your nose, and then I'll blow your shed apart with a grenade," George replied with that quiet air of his.

"Seventy'll be just fine," the undertaker agreed. "Leave it inside."

As they walked off, the exhausted Mrs. Svejk murmured, "Thanks."

"My name is George—George Smith. And you?"

"Heloise Svejk."

"Are you hungry, ma'am?"

"Very hungry and very thirsty."

"Come and have a hamburger with me at Harry's Bar."

"Thank you, but won't it be rather expensive?"

"No problem."

For a moment, George had actually thought about how slim his finances were. You have to understand that soldiers weren't being paid as much as they had been just after the Second World War, when a martini at Harry's Bar in Venice went for fifty cents. At the time we are speaking of, soldiers were paid very little, and a martini cost thirty dollars. But Harry usually gave credit, and it was the only place they could possibly go.

The bar was right around the corner. Nobody was there except for Harry, behind the counter. The place was very clean, it was cool, and nothing smelled.

"Hello, Private Smith, how are you?"

George couldn't figure out how Harry always remembered his name. Maybe it was because of all the money he owed him.

"Fine, thank you, Harry. Can we get something to eat?"

They sat at the corner table on the right, by the door. Harry brought two frosty martinis and two large glasses of ice water.

"I've got some marvelous caviar that just arrived from Iran. Would you like to start with that?"

George glanced at Mrs. Svejk. "Sure, why not!" he said.

George realized at once that Mrs. Svejk was a real lady. She was sipping her second martini and ate the caviar with utter indifference, as if she had been nibbling at it for hours on end.

"Fantastic!" George exclaimed. He thought the caviar was fantastic, and he thought it was fantastic that he was there with Heloise.

"It is good," she agreed.

They ordered lobster thermidor, and Harry poured the Chablis into a chilled carafe. George felt rather dizzy, and Mrs. Svejk smiled at him for the first time.

"You're a good person," she said.

"And you're beautiful. You are the most beautiful woman I've ever seen."

"Don't be silly!"

"No, I mean it."

END OF CHAPTER TWO

INTERMEZZO
BETWEEN CHAPTERS
TWO AND THREE

Dear Abelard,

Here is the first part of the manuscript of my first novel. I think it's an achievement that I got this far. I don't think it's too bad, and I'm sure that if I showed it to my cousin Wanda she would swoon as soon as she got to the part about the tug in love with the pilot boat. I only put that into the book to satisfy your natural predilection for thinking and saying stupid things. Wanda would say that the bearded man's desire to hold the tugboat in his hands is just one of the deviations that the French psychologist Lacan so efficiently described.

As you know, I used to see a lot of him. Whenever he saw me, he would say, "Oh, comme vous êtes gentil!" The only reason was that I had helped him ship a Murano-glass vase (or maybe it was a lamp, I don't remember) to one of his incidental concubines.

This Lacan always traveled with a large retinue. He was larger than life, and he was fully conscious of the fact, which is why he did so many strange things. At ten o'clock one morning he came into the lobby of the Cipriani Hotel in his underpants, as if it were the most natural thing in the world. He just wanted to infuriate the hotel manager, whom he couldn't stand. But he was perfectly fine with us. The only out-of-the-way thing he ever did in the years I knew him was to let out an inhuman howl one evening at dinner at Harry's Bar in Venice.

"Silence!" he wailed.

I think he was rather disappointed that no one took the slightest notice of him. People just went on talking. Which is fairly normal. I mention this for the benefit of anyone who might take it into his head to show off when I am around. And that includes you, of course.

To get back to my cousin Wanda—and may her psychologist rest in peace, that's one woman I'm glad I never met. She deserves a place in the *Guinness Book of World Records* for making my cousin do more stupid things than anybody in the world. I remember once when Wanda and I went sailing together on Lake Garda just off Torri del Benaco. We were both sixteen at the time. I saw the blond hairs poking out from the crotch of her bathing suit, and I was terribly upset. You see, I had intended to become a priest, but at that moment I realized I could never observe the vow of lifelong chastity. Since I was a young man of principle, I would have to give up the idea of becoming a priest, and it was all her fault. We slept in the same room that summer and, for some reason I never understood, before turning out the lights she would show me how good she was at belly dancing. The result was that I didn't get any sleep but daydreamed all kinds of wicked, indecent things. She really was good, so good that if she had decided to dance in the souk in Tangiers, instead of teaching Latin in Verona, she would have made a name for herself, and a lot of money as well.

Wanda gave me a detailed description of every sensation she felt in her lower groin the first time a fellow in Verona kissed her on the neck. If it hadn't been for my strict Catholic upbringing and all the incredible stories I had been told about cousins needing a papal dispensation, I would have been delighted to make a pass, even without the Vatican's approval. And may lightning strike me if she wouldn't have liked it too. What a lightning bolt I missed!

END OF THE INTERMEZZO
BETWEEN CHAPTERS
TWO AND THREE

CHAPTER THREE

In which the friendship of George and Heloise reaches a crucial point.

"Where do you come from?" Heloise asked.

"I'm from Alabama, and you?"

"Czechoslovakia."

George had a sudden urge to tell her his life story. The martinis and the wine had something to do with it. He told her about his father and his brickyard. George's mother had died of cancer, and his bereaved father thereupon married a dancer. He died soon after, a happy man. He had a heart attack on a houseboat, where he spent Saturdays and Sundays copulating like a teenager from dawn till dusk, the few Saturdays and Sundays he had left to live. But neither George nor his father had ever been in love.

George told her he was twenty-two, and how after graduation from high school he had joined the United States Army. He didn't know why—at least not until this morning, when he thought that maybe what his minister used to say wasn't all nonsense, and maybe there was some truth in what he said about the inscrutable ways of God's providence. Because ever since he laid eyes on Heloise for the first time, all aquiver in her high-heeled evening shoes (he didn't say this to her, and in fact he wondered why she was wearing evening shoes), he knew at last why he was in Lebanon. If she had been Jewish, he would have joined the Israeli army at once. If she had been an Arab or a Russian, he would have been just as willing to serve in Libya or in the Carpathians. All he needed was to look at her for the rest of his days. He understood at last that he had not come all this way to save Lebanon from the seventh invasion of the Jews or to turn back the thirteenth revolution of the Christians. Nor was he there to be the object of the paranoia of the brothers of their brothers. The only reason he was there was to avoid the terrible misfortune of Heloise suddenly disappearing—like a light going out in an instant. All the light in the world. He had at long last understood. There had been another reason too, even before this wonderful meeting: to save Harry's Bar and wonderful Harry as well.

"Harry!" he shouted. "The check!"

Harry came over with a sheet of paper in his hand. This is what it said:

Dear Pvt. Smith,
As of yesterday you owed me sixteen thousand dollars, and you still owe it to me. But today, if you don't mind, I want you to be my guest.
                              Harry Cipriani

Harry did not usually look at women customers for their beauty, but he too was struck by Heloise, and made what was a totally unusual gesture for him. The verb *treat* was not in his vocabulary. But Harry thought that at a time when his best-looking customers were Arafat Jr. and Qaddafi III, a woman like this deserved special treatment.

Private Smith looked Harry in the eye and had trouble getting up from the table, because he was very tired and he had had quite a bit to drink.

"You're a great man, Harry!" he said. "Would you have a room?"

"Sure, there's one free on the top floor."

"I want it now!"

"How long will you be staying?"

"How long do you think?"

"I rent rooms for a minimum of two weeks, although you're free to leave even after an hour."

"Then I'll stay two weeks."

"Fine, Private Smith. I'll show you to the room. Any luggage?"

"No luggage. Just her."

George turned to Heloise and smiled. The smile she gave him back was indescribable; it was sadder than sadness itself. That was when he realized he was terribly in love.

END OF CHAPTER THREE

INTERMEZZO
BETWEEN CHAPTERS
THREE AND FOUR

Dear Abelard,

The advantage the author has over the reader is that he knows everything his characters do, and he can decide what to tell and what not to tell. The reader has to settle for whatever the author thinks he should know.

The reason I say this is that, knowing your erotic penchant, I'm sure you have already turned ahead in the book to see what happened when our heroes, Heloise and George, went into the room on the top floor over Harry's Bar. The truth of the matter is that even I don't know everything they did. And words alone would not suffice. At the very least I would have to borrow images, sounds, words, and deeds from my film-director brother-in-law. He is famous for his erotic movies, and the experts consider him tops in the field.

I really hope that someday this story is filmed; then we can see all the things I haven't described. What I can tell you is that everything I know I heard from Harry in

Beirut. He had to keep George's presence a secret from his wife. She would not have approved, because the whole family knew George never paid his bill. So Harry told his wife that he rented the room first to the Tolmezzo Mountain-Climbing Association, then to touring drummers from Detroit, the Vienna Philharmonic Orchestra, and finally Arafat Jr. with four odalisques. Harry had to say something to account for all the noise and laughter that rang down four stories from the room where George and Heloise were staying. Sometimes you could even hear them over all the commotion in the bar, which happened to be full of American sailors at the time, because the Sixth Fleet was on shore leave. One evening an armoire fell over with such a crash that the lights downstairs went out. Sitting at the bar was Count Guillon, a handsome aristocrat from Treviso who was totally deaf. He pointed to the ceiling and winked. "Mice!"

Before retiring for the night, Harry would put fourteen bottles of cabernet outside the door of the room, two bottles of port, half a dozen shrimp sandwiches and half a dozen chicken. And he would remove the dirty dishes from the day before. Occasionally he listened for further sound from the room, but for some reason all he ever heard was joyous laughter. Things went on like that for two weeks.

One day the MPs came looking for a certain Private George Smith. Harry did not want to lose his license, so he said he didn't know the man; he'd never even seen him. George had been reported missing in action, and his aunt in Alabama, his mother's sister and a war widow herself, had been duly notified. It had been recommended that George be awarded the highest honor given to US soldiers shot down by Radical Party snipers.

The formalities were unusually rapid, because they wanted to have the ceremony before the gubernatorial primaries; it was meant to give a touch of class to the incumbent's campaign.

I have something else to say about Harry's hearing George and Heloise laugh. That's what makes me think there was something very special about them. Laughter is not the usual way men and women express their utter happiness at the culminating moment of you-know-what. They usually groan or wail or moan. And it is generally believed that the weepier the moan, the greater the satisfaction. But I've never been altogether convinced that was true. And the proof is that when George and Heloise came to climax, instead of moaning the way most people do, they laughed with joy. That's what I think the laughter Harry heard was probably about.

I'm not joking when I tell you something I actually witnessed when my father and I were running a hotel in Asolo. A lucious South American woman and a noble-man from Milan occasionally came to stay. They would go to their room, and after a while it was impossible to decide whether the noise that could even be heard in the lobby of the Sole Hotel a mile away was the South American woman cooing with love or a hefty contralto warming up her vocal cords.

They came rather often, and soon the whole town knew about their audio performance. When they came through the door of the hotel, the bar would already be full of fans hoping to make a night of it with a cup of coffee. After a few minutes of silent preliminaries, the sounds would start up. One listener was an elderly Greek teacher and a music lover, and when the couple upstairs started their concertizing, he would exclaim to himself: "Sublime, marvelous. What resonance!"

The first act usually lasted about an hour, and then the audience would take a stroll in the garden and comment on the performance. When the Milanese nobleman made his rather bewildered way down the stairs after the second act, he would often be greeted by applause and congratulations. One afternoon old Signora Noemi, a charming centenarian accompanied by her eighty-year-old daughter, even tried to give him a kiss.

There must have been a terrific struggle in that room—I mean the room that George and Heloise shared—because Harry told me it took two architects, seventeen carpenters, a plumber, and an electrician more than two months to get everything back in order. Which made George's bill that much higher.

END OF THE INTERMEZZO
BETWEEN CHAPTERS
THREE AND FOUR

CHAPTER FOUR

In which George and Heloise finally leave the room and go out into the world.

About ten o'clock one morning, exactly two weeks after George rented the room, the two of them came down the stairs and walked into the bar. Harry greeted them quite naturally and asked if they would like some coffee. George ordered double coffee for two.

George and Heloise seemed perfectly happy, to judge by their incredibly radiant glances. They didn't utter a word the whole time they sat in the bar; they were absorbed in thought.

Heloise had lost a bit of her tan, and George's face seemed drawn but rested. Harry continued in silence to polish his gleaming counter. He lifted the bottles one by one, dusted them, and put them back.

George got up and said, "Harry, we're leaving. Would you get me the bill?"

"Here it is. I drew it up in advance." He set the bill in front of George.

George signed it and told Harry to send it to his wealthy aunt in Alabama. "I'll write down the address for you."

Harry said that he already had the address. He didn't think it proper to forward the bill. He didn't even have the heart to tell George that he had been reported killed in action.

"Thanks for everything, Harry. See you soon."

"Good-bye, Private Smith. Good-bye, madam." Harry held the door for them, and there was a sudden gust of very dry torrid air.

George and Heloise stepped out into the dusty street. There was an unearthly calm, as if the city had suddenly died. The only sound was a car horn in the distance, and then silence. George put his arm around Heloise's waist, and the two of them slowly ambled down the street. When they got to the corner, George noticed a jeep parked across the street. There was an American soldier at the wheel. George went over to him and said, "Hi, Tom."

"Hi, George," the soldier replied.

"Do you mind if I take the jeep, buddy?"

"When will I get it back?"

"Maybe never."

"OK." Tom owed George a lot of favors. "Whenever you like."

Tom got out of the jeep, bowed to George, and helped Heloise get in.

"She's beautiful," Tom said.

"Forget it." George smiled.

"See you soon."

George turned the key and the engine started to belch. He put it into first gear, and the jeep moved forward, raising a cloud of dust behind. They took the first right and headed for the hills. Tom ran to the corner and watched them drive away until the cloud of dust behind them disappeared on the far horizon.

END OF CHAPTER FOUR

INTERMEZZO
BETWEEN CHAPTERS
FOUR AND FIVE

Dear Abelard,

As I said before, the author's great advantage is that he knows exactly what his characters are doing, and he can choose what to tell and what not to tell. But there is no denying that the reader may have an even greater advantage. He can stop reading whenever he wants to, regretting only that he has wasted his money.

But you have always had so little money that you would probably have nothing to do except go on reading, even if you wanted to stop. That's why I am writing to you. I certainly wouldn't ask you for advice or suggestions about what George and Heloise should do, because I know perfectly well what they are going to do. I just wanted to draw your attention to a couple of things that occurred to me as I was narrating this very unusual love story. You will have noticed that Heloise took it for granted that George would pay for dinner and the hotel. That certainly wouldn't go down well with the feminists, because no self-respecting women's-libber would accept such a patently ambiguous situation.

My sister-in-law Ornella, for example, is not, strictly speaking, a feminist. She has reasons of her own for insisting that she is liberated, though she really isn't. She would have insisted on paying her share of the bill, and that would have put Harry in the embarrassing position of taking cash payment for only half the check. The funny part is that if my sister-in-law had been in Heloise's place, especially after a couple of drinks, she would have been perfectly happy to indulge in erotic games with George. But her mania for paying her own way would have ruined everything before it even started. I don't know if you remember how beautiful my sister-in-law is—you always seem rather intimidated around my relatives; but believe me, she is one of the most beautiful women I have ever desired. But she has one terrible defect: she won't let anyone pay for her. Otherwise she might have become very rich by now, even richer than my cousin Wanda, provided of course that my cousin had become a belly dancer in the Tangiers souk instead of a Latin teacher in Verona.

In my short life I have met women far less attractive who have been paid a great deal of money even when they claimed to be making love just for the sake of love. Ever since the days when whorehouses were legal, I have had the utmost respect for women who calmly offer a remedy for lust in exchange for money. When I was a youth, there were marvelous professionals who could satisfy any man who ended up between their legs. You are too young to remember them, but those houses were full of human warmth and kindness. If you never knew them you have missed out on something really important in terms of the spirit and the flesh alike.

We used to play tricks to frighten the priests and old married gentlemen who came on the sly, like setting off the alarm bell that meant the police were about to raid. But pranks aside, believe me when I say that a night spent there, and maybe the next morning as well, with the occasional game of billiards thrown in, was a human experience I wouldn't have missed for all the tea in China.

We set off the alarm bell hundreds of times, but in all those years I never saw the police come even once.

END OF THE INTERMEZZO
BETWEEN CHAPTERS
FOUR AND FIVE

CHAPTER FIVE

In which Tom Margitai has some doubts and George and Heloise stop to rest on their journey by jeep.

Private Tom Margitai decided to stay and watch as the cloud of dust raised by the jeep slowly grew smaller on the horizon and finally vanished completely.

Watching things until the very end was a mania of Tom's, and every time he did so, he had the same thought: if he didn't watch till the end, he would not live long enough to have another chance to do it again. He couldn't have cared less about the jeep; it was already the fourth he had lost that week. The first two blew up while he was off buying cigarettes; the third one blew a tire, so he left it on the side of the road. Every time he went back to headquarters to get another one, the duty officer had nothing to say. He simply gave a weary nod by way of indicating that Tom could take his pick of the enormous collection that was always parked on the wharf at the port. For that matter, Tom was glad to have done George a favor, because the last time they'd gone to Harry's Bar, George had sponsored ten rounds of Bellinis, the most expensive drink you could order there. Tom of course knew that George had been reported killed in action. At first he was sorry he hadn't said something to his friend, but then he decided that it was probably just as well he hadn't, seeing the company George was in. In fact, he decided then and there that he wouldn't tell a soul he had seen George on the street that morning, and in the best of health, to judge by the way he looked.

Meanwhile, George was driving happily along the twisting curves of the hills. The sky was a deep blue, the kind you often have in Lebanon, and the air turned cooler as they gradually went up. Just around a curve he saw a beautiful sloping meadow dotted with cedar trees. He pulled up on the side of the road and looked in the rear for the survival supplies that every good soldier of the United States of America ought to carry with him in a vehicle. He found them in a plastic bag. There was canned meat, crackers, a tin of sardines, a can of ham, a can of spinach and another one of beans, two cans of Coca-Cola, and six aspirins. There was also a bottle of Booth's gin, which was not standard issue but must have been part of Tom's unfailing personal stock. George gave silent thanks to Tom and asked Heloise, "Shall we have a bite?"

She smiled at him. The sadness was gone from Heloise's face. Her mouth opened to reveal her sparkling teeth, and her eyes, deep turquoise now, squeezed shut to share in the joyous delight of her face. George felt as if he had been physically struck by a violent, impulsive rush of affection. He looked at her too, in the same way, and then he gave her a very tender kiss, his lips barely brushing against hers.

He took the bag out of the jeep, and some ten yards away he sat down on the sloping green meadow. She got out and followed him, moving unsteadily on the high heels of her evening shoes, the ones she wore the first time they met, the shoes that did so much to heighten that incredible quivering stride of hers. As he watched her approach, a small gust of wind lifted some dry leaves from the ground. It moved forward in that strange, bizarre way that little whirlwinds have in the grasslands in North Africa, and it came toward her, the only movement in the still afternoon air. The little whirlwind lingered a moment at Heloise's side. The leaves it had sucked up from the ground spun lightly and rapidly in a shaft at its center. Then the dust devil decided to hit her, slightly disturbing the shreds of her dress and her long black hair, which now seemed to have a brighter sheen, perhaps from happiness.

It seemed to George—indeed, he was absolutely sure—that nature had marshaled all the delicacy it could just to give Heloise an exquisitely tender caress.

END OF CHAPTER FIVE

INTERMEZZO
BETWEEN CHAPTERS
FIVE AND SIX

Dear Abelard,

I can imagine you already have your doubts about that little whirlwind caressing Heloise. As a matter of fact, I remember that I didn't believe it either the first time I heard of it, but then I experienced it myself. Twice, in fact.

The first time was in Morocco.

I had stopped in the open countryside—it was a bright November day without a breath of wind, and I wanted to take a close, careful look at one of those rare landscapes you see only in Africa. The landscape stretching out for hundreds and hundreds of miles looks like a mere patch in the clearest sky you can imagine. You get the feeling that the whole world is spread out before you, naked as the day the gods made it. Well, suddenly, as if a spirit had come out of nowhere, some dry leaves in a green meadow started spinning around in an eddy on the ground. The leaves spun faster and faster and started rising from the ground until they were caught up in a spiral that must have been six feet high. This dust devil moved slowly from place to place, and everywhere it went it gathered up new leaves and new strength. And then, just as suddenly as it had sprung up, it dropped to the ground and died out. It left me with the oddest sensation of having been present at the mysterious revelation of one small secret of the world.

The second time was in Kenya, the land of Adam. There is a solemnity about everything in that country, from the long, smooth slopes of the mountains to the gentle surge of the wind, from the swift, silent lope of the giraffes to the aloof, detached glance of the lions.

Late one January afternoon, after driving for several hours along a rough dirt track, I was beginning to think I would never again see a place inhabited by human beings. And then, just around a bend in the road, I came upon an unexpected sight.

Down below, an enormous dry salt lake stretched to the foot of the hill I was on. In the distance, the brilliant green slopes of Kilimanjaro marked the far edge of the world. Dozens of little whirls were spinning across the broad expanse. The whitish funnels of dust varied in tone, bright on the side that was lighted by the setting sun and dark on the side caught by advancing night. Each vortex must have been sixty feet high. They moved slowly around the plain in no apparent direction, and everywhere they passed they tossed up small stones and pebbles. One of the vortices was bolder than the rest and ran straight through a herd of resting buffalo, but not one of the animals moved or even took notice of nature's extravaganza.

So believe me when I say that the story of Heloise's dust whirl is perfectly plausible, because there are areas of the world where you are in closer touch with the ultimate source of things, and very often something spiritual hovers about things human.

END OF THE INTERMEZZO
BETWEEN CHAPTERS
FIVE AND SIX

CHAPTER SIX

In which Heloise lunches in a meadow with George and begins to speak.

"If I were a mountain," Heloise remarked pensively, "I would love you. I would love you even if I were a meadow, and if I were a little apple tree I would love you. I would love you forever if I were any of these things, because I'd always be there with nothing else to do but think about loving you."

"And what if you were Heloise?" George asked.

"But I am Heloise!" She smiled.

George was a very simple man and always wanted to know how things stood. "I thought you were a mountain, or rather a meadow or an apple tree."

"And if I were, would you love me?"

"You know what I'd do?"

"No."

"I'd climb up the mountain, tiptoe across the meadow as quiet as I could, and then I'd eat the apples."

"And then?"

"And then . . ." He broke off. Looking at her, he realized that he had never seen her speak with her mouth full as she was doing now. He decided that she was even more desirable when she spoke with her mouth full. And when the right moment came he would ask her always to make sure her mouth was full before she said anything. His next thought was that this must mean he was in love, because if he had seen anyone else but Heloise speak with a full mouth, all he would have felt was a twinge of irritation.

Which is why George stopped after that "And then"; but his mouth was also full, and Heloise said she liked him even more with his mouth full. The two of them laughed until the tears streamed down, the way only lovers can laugh at the incredibly idiotic things they say when they are in love.

Heloise turned serious and said, "George, look at me."

George still had tears in his eyes from laughing so hard. But he too turned serious and replied, "Yes, Heloise."

The intense look they exchanged was their promise to love each other till death did them part. Then Heloise told George she wanted to use the seventy dollars from the coffin to buy herself something to wear. George said they could go to the nearby village, where, among other things, there was a merchant who gave credit. So they got back into the jeep and soon reached a small village that was actually more a market than a village. They had some difficulty fording a stream, and then George parked the jeep outside a tent circled by baskets full of black olives. It was hot again, and there was a strong smell of sweat and spices everywhere. Shouting children stormed the jeep, and all the merchants seemed to know George. What was odd was that he owed them a great deal of money, but no one seemed at all angry. Indeed, they greeted him very effusively and offered him everything they had in their stalls.

That was George. There was something immediately likable about him, and it was so strong that it leveled any barrier. He moved among the crowd greeting everyone. He nodded at the women and listened patiently to everything the men had to say. He was like a chief back from a long journey to distant parts. Finally he and Heloise stopped in front of a little store that sold fabrics of all colors. She picked out three dresses and he bought two brightly colored djellabas. He put one on over his uniform to the great amusement of the children.

Heloise went into a tent and came out wearing a long red shawl wound tightly around her body. She walked up and down, slightly aquiver, like a professional model. The sight of her beauty was like a punch in the stomach to George, and he turned pale with emotion.

The merchants and their women crowded around George and Heloise. The two of them were enveloped by a vast array of sparkling teeth, a universal smile of utter admiration. Then Heloise started to dance. All her quivering ceased. Her body seemed barely to touch the ground, and this made an extremely deep impression on everyone. No one could remember ever seeing someone dance like that, not even the elders who had spent years traveling the deserts, oases, and palm groves of the world.

Heloise danced for more than an hour, but no one

was aware of time passing; not a word was uttered, no one sat down or stood up, no one looked at sky or earth—such was the delicate grace of the beautiful Heloise. Toward the end, she held out her hand to George, and he joined in her dance. For many years to come, everyone remembered that sunny afternoon when George and Heloise stopped to shop and dance.

END OF CHAPTER SIX

INTERMEZZO
BETWEEN CHAPTERS
SIX AND SEVEN

Dear Abelard,

You are a very inquisitive person, and I imagine you have already asked yourself several times how there could ever be a Harry's Bar in Beirut in the year 2000. You have the same kind of mind as those Italian movie-critics who could find nothing better to say about that marvelous Milos Forman film *Amadeus* than that its story of Mozart and Salieri wasn't true, or at least not likely. I really don't know why I decided to write all these things to you, why I picked you out of all my friends, since you are the one with the least imagination and the least flexible mind.

Anyhow, whether you believe it or not, there actually was a Harry's Bar in Beirut in the year 2000. The owner was Harry Cipriani, and he was the son of Giuseppe, who was the son of Arrigo, who was the son of another Giuseppe. Harry was the tenth son of the first-mentioned Giuseppe, who had married fifteen times, and who reaped so much from his divorces he could have lived in the lap of luxury for six generations. But not Giuseppe; he invested his whole fortune in ten bars around the world. He put one of his sons to work in each of them. The sons were all named Harry—that way nobody could ever say the bar wasn't Harry's. The funny thing was that all of Giuseppe's sons looked very much alike; they all seemed to be the spitting image of great-grandfather Giuseppe, who founded the first Harry's Bar, the one in Venice, in Italy. I hope your unbelieving provincial curiosity is satisfied once and for all.

There is one thing I forgot to mention, in the part of the novel where I said that while George and Heloise were four floors above Harry's Bar making love for all they were worth, downstairs there were sailors of the United States Sixth Fleet on special leave. There was a time—I remember it very clearly—when in the wake of student unrest in France in 1968, special concessions were being made to young people all over the world, so the United States Navy allowed its men to wear civilian clothes while off duty. That is what the US Navy offered its sailors, while terrorism was heating up in Europe, and university professors were being humiliated in China during the Cultural Revolution. At the same time, Russia was filling up its insane asylums with dissidents—all those people, with Solzhenitsyn in the lead, who wrote or openly declared that after fifty years they were tired of waiting for the revolution bus to arrive.

This business of American sailors in civilian clothes lasted about ten years, the ultimate symbol of what the United States of America could dream up in the area of dissent.

This probably doesn't seem like much to you, but for us saloonkeepers, among others, this change in behavior had enormous significance.

To begin with, none of us—I am speaking of barmen—had any concrete way now of determining before a brawl started how quarrelsome a sailor might be. Let me explain. When the uniform was obligatory, it gave you a good idea of the sailor wearing it. Chevrons on the upper arm indicated the sailor's rank—I am talking about sailors below the rank of warrant officer. The lowest rank was one chevron, then two, and then three. So far so good. Stripes on the forearm indicated years of service. One stripe for four years, two for eight, three for twelve, and four for sixteen years. If a sailor had two chevrons, say, and three service stripes, or twelve years, you knew you had a potential troublemaker on your hands. That's because every time a sailor was in a brawl, the navy took one chevron away. So if you calculated chevrons and service stripes, it wasn't hard to figure out with whom you were dealing.

At the time uniforms were mandatory, I remember, there were sailors with twenty years of service who had only one chevron. It was worth making friends with them at once, the minute they set foot on land, because either they were perfect idiots or they were the kind who flared up at the slightest provocation. You couldn't take such precautions when they were out of uniform— not to mention the awful taste the sailors had in choosing their "civilian" uniforms. That is a prerogative of all the armies and navies in the world. A soldier or a sailor is always in uniform, even when wearing civilian clothes. You have to have spent thirty years in a bar to grasp these subtleties. For example, you can tell right away when a civilian gets into a uniform. Mussolini looked like a marionette in uniform, while Hitler looked like a prisoner in civvies. Some people are born military, and others are born civilians. People ought to wear their proper uniforms all the time. (George had certainly stayed civilian, and so he would remain all his life.)

Another prerogative of sailors is that they always imitate their captain. There are good ships and bad ships, depending on who the captain is. I remember very clearly one time in the 1960s when the crew of an American cruiser, the *Des Moines*, came ashore in Venice on special leave. Aside from the hundreds of liters of alcohol a few hundred sailors managed to down in one week at Harry's Bar, what really impressed me was the extremely good manners they all had. They had a gentlemanliness about them they never lost, even in a state of drunkenness.

I remember that to keep those I had stopped serving from trying to get a drink elsewhere, I would temporarily confiscate the wallet of anyone who was drunk. At a certain point there were two hundred sailors' wallets in the safe. The crewmen would come back every half-hour, unsteady on their feet, trying to prove they were no longer drunk; but if I wasn't totally sure, I'd keep them off the liquor for three or four hours at least.

Even the troublemakers in that crew had their own way of making trouble. Before trading punches they always took off the blue kerchief around their neck so that the good name of the US Navy would not be tarnished in the brawl. Without the kerchief, of course, they could not strictly be considered in uniform.

Maybe it was because they had seen the world, or maybe it was because their skipper came from an aristocratic Boston family, but the fact remains that I have a wonderful memory of that crew. One evening a member of the crew, a sailor with twenty years' service and two chevrons, got completely drunk and sat down at the table of an elderly Venetian countess. She was the daughter of a jeweler of French descent, and she was famous for her snobbery. She had such a good time that she invited him back to her palazzo on the Grand Canal. He was a very good-looking man, by the way, and they stayed together until the cruiser left.

This letter may seem a bit long, but I'd like to tell you something else about uniforms, something that happened a few years ago in Jamaica. You might think it pure fantasy, but I saw it all with my own eyes.

Well, one very bright sunny morning on a path along the coast of Jamaica, as I mentioned, two middle-aged men and two middle-aged women dressed in tennis-player uniforms met four young men in priest uniforms. The tennis players raised their weapons, that is to say their rackets, with weary enthusiasm by way of greeting, and the priests responded by making the sign of the cross with their right hand.

The four young priests were on their way to a nearby church to celebrate a solemn high mass in memory of the body and soul of an old general of the past regime, and a few minutes later they ran into four teenagers wearing hippie uniforms. The hippies gestured insultingly at the priests, albeit not without some embarrassment, and the priests responded by lifting their hands and eyes to heaven to beg the forgiveness of somebody-up-there in God-uniform.

The four hippies sat down under a coconut palm, and when they finished the last of a marijuana joint, they wearily got to their feet. They straggled bleary-eyed along the beach in the direction of the nearby town of Ocho Rios. On the way they were stopped by four men in lifeguard uniforms who greeted them, as it were, by waving their rakes threateningly. The hippies responded with obscene gestures and ran off toward a nearby hill.

The four lifeguards continued lazily raking the sand until four people emerged from the green lawn behind the palm trees lining the edge of the shore: two aged women and two aged men in the uniform of rich aged bathers. The two aged men took out their wallets and offered a tip by way of greeting, and the four lifeguards dropped their rakes and rushed to set out the beach chairs for sunning. The four aged people began carefully applying sun lotion. They kindly greased one another's back, because they couldn't have done it for themselves. Then, fearing a glimpse of some flash or sign that might indicate the sudden approach of a frightful final reckoning, they lay back and rather apprehensively watched the far horizon that separated sky and sea.

Instead of a bolt of divine lightning, they were very delighted and relieved to see the approach of four little sails, swift and light as the bright wings of flying swallows. The white plastic boards supporting the sails lightly skimmed the surface of the water carrying four youths in surfer uniform. An elegant maneuver brought them onto the shore. They laughed and joked among themselves excessively, perhaps because they felt observed, and began dismantling their Windsurfers. The four aged people saluted them with a wave of their straw hats, full of admiration and some regret as well, and the surfers replied with a display of dazzling white teeth in striking contrast to the bronzed faces that emerged from jet black wet suits.

Bursting with health and vigor, the four surfers were loading their gear onto the roof of a broken-down jalopy when four policemen in police uniforms gunned their four bright red motorcycles around a turn in the road. The four policemen dismounted and with no greeting at all asked the four surfers why there was no license plate on the front of the car. They did not wait for a reply before slowly removing their left glove, taking off one finger at a time with the thumb and index finger of the right hand. All the joyous, effervescent vitality that had enveloped the four surfers disappeared as if by magic.

As soon as the surfers were served with the ticket, the policemen put on their helmets, mounted their motorcycles, and drove off in orderly file without forcing the engines. It was not long before they had to apply the brakes, because they were amazed to see something quite unprecedented just beyond the low wall dividing the road from the beach. They saw four strikingly beautiful young women in nudist uniform. Of course, there was a perfectly good reason for this: the girls were doing a film about nudists. The policemen would hear none of it, however, because nude uniforms were against the law. The four girls were arrested and had to get on the rear seat of the motorcycles uniformed just as they were. They were taken to jail in Ocho Rios.

This is where the story ends. I can already imagine the corrupt glint in your eye, since you would like to know what happened next. All I can tell you is that I witnessed the arrest, but I was not present when the eight of them reached the jail. Indeed, the next day I asked what happened to the girls, and I was told that the only person confined in the Ocho Rios jailhouse was an old drunk. No one else had been in jail there for the past ten years.

END OF THE INTERMEZZO
BETWEEN CHAPTERS
SIX AND SEVEN

CHAPTER SEVEN

In which the High Command of the American armed forces in Lebanon discovers that George Smith is alive and well.

At three in the afternoon on August 9, General John Custer, commander in chief of the Expeditionary Peace Corps of the United States of America in Lebanon, was puffing a Romeo and Juliet at the desk of what had been the command room. Behind him a smiling portrait of President Reagan II looked over the heads of the visitors who usually entered that room. A door to his right led to the private bathroom, which was not in service because there had been no water for a week. The main door in front of him was closed, and there was an enormous, gaping hole in the wall to his left—the result of tank shelling by the Christian Liberation forces—where his secretary Suzy's desk had been until two days before. The hole in the fourth-floor wall provided the general with an unobstructed view of the tumultuous traffic along the Avenue des Anglais, and as usual the chaotic noise was loud and clear.

Custer had just come back to the office after lunching on marvelous green cannelloni at Harry's Bar. He had spent an amusing half-hour admiring Harry's skill in preparing fifteen martinis at once. The cigar was an after-lunch gift from Arafat Jr., who was always well supplied with original Cuban products.

General Custer was at peace with himself. In a phone conversation a few minutes earlier, he had offered his condolences to the general in command of the Italian expeditionary corps, who was grieving because a missile had blown up his arsenal. Fortunately no one had been on guard at the time, so there were no casualties. Nice fellows those Italians, Custer thought, but they did take everything too seriously. Custer was a Vietnam veteran and knew that what was essential in the military was to do only what was . . . essential. By following this rule he had become a highly respected officer, and what's more, he was still alive after all those years at war.

There was a knock on the door. "Come in!" he said.

"Lieutenant Ryland reporting, sir."

He couldn't stand this Ryland—a little chap with gold-rimmed glasses who looked like a bookkeeper—and forever fretted in disapproval of his work. Among other things, Ryland always picked the worst moment to arrive, and every time he appeared he brought bad news. It was Custer's impression that Ryland wore an impassive expression on his face to mask the sadistic pleasure he took in announcing catastrophe.

"What is it?" Custer asked impatiently.

"May I call in Private Tom Margitai? He has something interesting to report, General, sir."

"What is it about?"

"Private George Smith."

"Well?"

"They found him."

"Eh?"

"Yes sir, General."

"Alive?"

"Yes sir, General."

"Wounded?"

"Seems not, sir."

"Where is he now?"

"May I call Private Margitai in now, sir?"

"Come in!"

Tom came in followed by two military police.

"Who are you?" General Custer asked them.

"Sergeant Nobel and Sergeant Amundsen, sir."

"Speak up."

"We're responsible for the jeeps in the vehicle pool, and we noticed that Private Tom Margitai checked out five jeeps in less than a week."

"What do you have to say for yourself?" the general asked Tom.

"Two of them blew up, sir, one had a flat, and I'm driving the fifth one, sir."

"So, what's the problem?" the general asked.

"The fourth jeep, sir," Amundsen muttered.

"What fourth jeep?" It suddenly dawned on him then that one jeep was missing from Tom Margitai's story. "What happened to jeep number four?"

"I lent it to Private George Smith," Tom replied reluctantly. "He needed it."

"When?"

The general started feeling a bit uncomfortable. Something seemed to be out of kilter.

"July twenty-eighth, sir."

"But Smith died on July nineteenth!" Custer exclaimed.

There were two possibilities, he thought. Either this Margitai was lying because he sold the jeep, or they had made one of the biggest blunders of the war.

He had received a sympathy telefax from the President the day before, and he himself had penned a handwritten letter to Smith's aunt. If he was still alive, it could mean the end of Custer's career and early pension.

"If you've made this whole thing up, I'll put you behind bars for the rest of your life!"

Tom swallowed with difficulty and then said, "I assure you, General, sir, I saw George Smith on July twenty-eighth near Harry's Bar. He asked me for the jeep, and I gave it to him. I thought he was with military intelligence, so I didn't ask any questions."

"Was he alone?" the general asked.

"No sir."

"Whom was he with?"

"A woman."

"Ah!"

"A real looker, excuse me, sir."

Custer remained silent for more than a minute, his head in his hands and his elbows resting on the table. Then he said: "Listen, Private Margitai. If you don't bring Private George Smith back here within twenty-four hours, together with your goddam jeep and this beautiful girl, I'll have you up for court martial on grand larceny. Twenty years in jail, minimum. Now get out!"

"Yes sir, General, sir."

Tom went out in the custody of Nobel and Amundsen.

"What are you looking at?" Custer yelled at Ryland.

Ryland clicked his heels and got out as fast as he

could, leaving poor General Custer frowning with terrible thoughts.

The general suddenly stood up and went out, slamming the door behind him. He decided he would go to Suzy's. She would console him. He got behind the wheel of the first jeep he found in the courtyard and roared past the guard, who disappeared in the dust he raised in passing.

Near the Avenue de la Liberté he got caught in a horrible traffic jam. He was stuck for half an hour trying to get rid of a gang of kids who wanted to trade him pistol bullets for chocolate bars. He finally reached the outskirts of Beirut and drove past a row of little houses on a little cedar-lined street. He drew up outside a little white villa, got out of the jeep, and rang the bell. Suzy opened the door. She had come from the swimming pool behind the house and was wearing a beach robe. A large breast, still moist, was visible between its pink lapels. They embraced, and Suzy asked, "What's the matter, General? You look depressed."

He took her arm and drew her into the garden.

John Custer sank into a cane chair and said, "Get me a whiskey sour, will you?"

Suzy prepared a giant whiskey sour with lots of ice, sat down beside him, and softly caressed his head. She listened patiently to the whole story that threatened to blow up in his face.

END OF CHAPTER SEVEN

INTERMEZZO
BETWEEN CHAPTERS
SEVEN AND EIGHT

Dear Abelard,

You'll have to admit that the reason I've got you to read this far is mainly your indolence, not to mention how irresistibly you are drawn by the subtle fascination of investigating, imagining, and reading any detail concerning what is ultimately the subject nearest to your heart: in a word, sex. But I have already told you that this sort of intimate detail was rarely if ever included in what I was told.

I can assure you, however, that George and Heloise—at least so I was told—made love practically every time they had a chance, which is to say any time they were alone long enough to attend to the almost spasmodic attraction that constantly brought them together.

That is all I can tell you for now. Besides, I am sure that their relations involved the normal abnormalities of normal love affairs. And I consider it pointless to discuss that sort of thing. I have never understood, for example, the point of basing the main theme of a film plot on the extremely boring and banal sexual performance of an aging Marlon Brando with a little brunette whose big hairy pubic triangle is easier for me to remember than her name. The movie was called *Last Tango in Paris* for purely contingent reasons, to make it seem Art Deco. I'll tell you quite frankly that I am afraid I actually missed what everyone told me was the most interesting scene, the butter scene, because I fell fast asleep right after the first exhausting carnal encounter, when Marlon Brando, who shouldn't have been subjected to that kind of stress at his age, made love standing up in his raincoat with the little brunette, who still had her fur coat on.

So there you have it. There are some things I prefer not to write about, though if anyone who lives for sex or earns a living from it should read this book and be curious to learn the details of what George and Heloise actually did together, I might be willing to oblige him— but only orally, just to teach him a thing or two that would convince him at once that the least he should do is change his business.

Getting back to the origin of Harry's Bar—even you have probably read that it was founded in Venice in 1931 by Giuseppe Cipriani, that he was my father, and that he was a genius in his line. And he probably would have been a genius in any other line he might have gone into, but he was not a genius in that particular field of endeavor known as high finance—anything but. It is true that I too, for example, am clearly a product of one kind of genius he had, because if he hadn't had a son, Harry's Bar would not have continued to exist, at least not in the same way we are trying to run it. It would

51

have become one more imitation of all the poor imitations there are around the world. As his son I should naturally have turned out to be the opposite of him; that is to say, I should have at least had a talent for being either very poor or very rich. This is the quality that, especially in recent years, has distinguished the figure of every honest and dishonest financier alike.

Instead, at least so far, I don't think there has been any substantial change in what I have.

What I am trying to tell you is that every partner our family has ever had has always cheated us in a very partnerly fashion—except for Harry Pickering, the man who financed Harry's Bar at the start. That was after he repaid a loan my father had given him after the crash in 1929, a loan without any collateral or guarantee, offered so that Pickering could get back to America.

Let me give you one example: my own. For many years I was an unpaid employee of my father's partners, and the only tangible recompense I received in the end was a fly-fishing rod manufactured by Hardy, the famous English company. The rod was made of Holycoona, a material that is only slightly less expensive than Palakoona, and I tried in vain to sell it for the modest sum of $100,000, which is what I thought I deserved for ten years of honest work. What irritated me most in the whole business is that, instead of giving me the finest rod available, they gave me one that when you take a close look is really quite mediocre.

But don't let that surprise you, because this kind of behavior was part and parcel of the modus operandi of the people who became my father's partners when he built the hotel on the Giudecca island in Venice. To give you another example: One of the lady partners decided to build herself a yacht designed by a great English marine architect. It seemed a little expensive, even if she was a millionaire, so she gave orders for it to be shortened a few feet to save a hundred thousand dollars or so. This made the yacht too short for the high seas, and every time she crossed the ocean there was a serious risk of sinking.

I also remember that this lady took a personal interest in provisioning the crew before every cruise, usually in the company of her second husband, an aging Czech gigolo and former RAF pilot. They would question me very carefully about the price of bottled beer, for example. They always preferred the brands that gave a deposit back to the slightly more expensive no-return brands. And they never ordered more than twenty bottles or so at a time, with a saving of maybe a couple of dollars. She thought very highly of me as a specialist in writing telegrams, because I often saved her a few words without changing the meaning of the messages. I have met a lot of poor people in my life, including you, the poorest of them all, but nobody whose poverty was worse than that of a great many rich people.

END OF THE INTERMEZZO
BETWEEN CHAPTERS
SEVEN AND EIGHT

CHAPTER EIGHT

In which General Custer continues his visit to Suzy, his secretary.

Suzy fixed herself a glass full of gin and tonic and sat on a small sofa by the general.

"So George Smith is alive?"

"Apparently alive and kicking."

"Where has he been all this time?"

"With some woman."

"Where?"

"I don't know."

Suzy suddenly broke out in the silvery laugh that had so often put him in a good humor. This time, however, it did not remove the worried expression from his face.

"So he's really not dead!"

"No," he replied gloomily.

"Not even wounded?"

"No."

"What are you going to do now?" Suzy asked.

"Hm. I've got to think. In any case, we've got to find him. Then we'll see."

"You mean, you still don't know where he is?"

"No."

"Who's looking for him?"

"Ryland."

"Oh Lord!"

"Exactly!"

Custer gulped down the rest of his whiskey sour. Suzy got up to fix him another. She thought he needed it. She came back and, handing it to him, said, "Darling!"

Suzy was wonderful. Custer always remembered the day she first knocked on the door of his office. He had said, "Yes," and she poked her head around the half-open door and asked, "May I come in?"

A vision, he thought. Maybe he was hallucinating. Then when she was all the way into the room, and he had taken in the rest of that marvelous body, he was moved to stand up. Hats off to beauty! And the senses!

He asked: "Whom do I have the pleasure . . . ?"

"The pleasure and honor are all mine, General Custer. I'm your new secretary. My name is Suzanne Sweet." Two hours later they were at her house sipping whiskey at poolside. He did not go back to headquarters until the following day.

He had heard all kinds of things about her. She had been to bed with almost everyone in the United States Army. She did, however, have one great gift. When you were with her, she made you forget the past at once, and you felt that as far as she was concerned, you were the only man in the whole world. A splendid creature.

He called her the faithless faithful Suzanne. As long as you blotted out the constant suspicion of betrayal, you could be perfectly happy with her. And he was—

when he wasn't overwhelmed by devastating waves of jealousy.

"Darling!" Suzy had said. And at that moment he was sure that her love was true, and that she truly understood him.

"I have to get back to headquarters," Custer said.

"I'll come too."

"Thanks."

"Thanks for what? This is when you really need a secretary!"

She dressed quickly in front of him. While he looked at her naked body, he thought of the prudishness of his wife, a Swiss woman he hadn't once in all their years seen with her girdle off. He silently cursed Ryland and tenderly kissed Suzy's cheek as they walked to the door.

They both got into the jeep. She slipped behind the wheel, backed out smoothly, and headed for town.

END OF CHAPTER EIGHT

INTERMEZZO
BETWEEN CHAPTERS
EIGHT AND NINE

Dear Abelard,

To give you some relief after so much abstinence, let me try to remind you what we were like—I won't say sexually, but epidermally at least—in the 1940s. Or rather, after 1945, the famous year of liberation, when millions of people still drew strength of spirit from looking to a magic future of miracles in a free and peaceful world without war or conflict. Everyone, and I mean everyone, was discovering the joy of loving others, forgetful of the fact that some years earlier a guy by the name of God had commanded, "Love thy neighbor as thyself." Except Fascists—although that had not, of course, been spelled out.

I remember from those days a friend of mine named Giorgio, a country gentleman with thick black hair slicked back with brilliantine who looked something like Rudolph Valentino and who waltzed backward like nobody else in the world. He used to invite us to his house every night, my sister and me and other friends. We used to tell my mother that we were going to Giorgio's to study, though she never believed us. She was rightly suspicious by nature, because for many years she had waited up nights in Verona for my railway engineer grandfather, who often came home at dawn quite soused and smelling of talcum powder after an evening of cheer in some house of pleasure. The smell of talcum powder lingered for days after. Of course, he grumbled that he had been up all night at a secret meeting of clandestine Socialists.

I discovered the existence of cabernet, which I guzzled lying on the magnificent sofas in Giorgio's house, and with the lights down low, I had little trouble sliding my hand under the sweater of a beautiful girl named Lia. At the same time, I tried to get used to the electrifying sensation of joining my tongue to hers. Getting my other hand under her skirt was out of the question. Partly it was because, by the time I got past the top of her slip and the obstruction of the needless bra and finally managed to brush the tip of my finger against one of her little nipples—wondering whether it really was the nipple or a large mole—Lia would be ashamed to have let things go so far and usually shoved me away. Her face would be red with emotion and frustrated desire. She would get up from the sofa nervously and put a record on the modern American record-player, while I, sated with conquest, gulped down the other half of the bottle. I would go out into the narrow streets of Venice, staggering slightly, my head and heart full of wonderful feelings and very noble intentions.

More marriages were arranged in Giorgio's house

than in any other place I know—including my own. Giorgio's is where I decided to marry my wonderful companion in life, the sister of my sister-in-law Ornella, and that's where Giorgio's own marriage and a host of others were decided as well. And I will never forget one evening when two people who had never seen each other before decided they were made for each other, just because she (her name was Patrizia) suddenly discovered that he (his name was Gigi) danced the boogie-woogie like, as we said in those days, a god.

I think that the difference between those not-so-far-off days and the present is the same as that between the sound of a Spitfire engine and the roar of a jet plane a few hundred feet overhead. There was something human about the sound of old planes, and we could imitate it. During the war we would make the sound in philosophy class; Professor Benedetti thought there really was an air raid, and he would make the whole class go down to the ground floor. The masters at this imitation were Storelli and Talamini but, with a bit of practice, all of us were able to do it with fairly credible results.

That is how things were in Italy between 1945 and 1950. Girls were still interested in getting married, and that conditioned the way they acted with the boys. So our only alternative was to visit the houses or go abroad. My father often sent me to England during the holidays to study English. He did not care much about where in England. I usually went to stay with customers, who acted one way in Italy and altogether differently at home. My first major impact with the byways of puritanism came one whole winter I spent within the walls of a grim castle set on the soft slopes of Somerset. Beds were always overpopulated, the excuse being that there were ghosts, and the only time you could get any sleep at all was during the day. To put it mildly, I made only slight progress in my studies that year.

END OF THE INTERMEZZO
BETWEEN CHAPTERS
EIGHT AND NINE

CHAPTER NINE

In which George and Heloise receive a visit from Tom Margitai accompanied by Lieutenant Ryland and Sergeants Amundsen and Nobel.

By seven in the morning, George had been awake for almost two hours. He had awakened with a start thinking Heloise was not there. Neither of them were deep sleepers. Just as it had been during the fourteen nights they spent upstairs from Harry's Bar, sleep was rather a lazy, drowsy, happy extension of waking reality. George felt the warmth of Heloise's body and then her delicate breathing. He adored knowing that she was sleeping by his side. It was almost like loving her in secret. The night before, they had dined at the home of the chief merchant of the village together with his whole family. The room they had been given upstairs for the past two weeks was large and bright, and the enormous bed was very comfortable.

He had been thinking ever since he woke up. He often woke up very early. He considered it the finest moment of the day. He lay quietly on his back and let his mind wander, enjoying the unusual clarity of his thoughts. He was trying to plan things in an orderly fashion. He thought that sooner or later he would have to write his aunt and tell her everything that had happened. She had loved him tenderly since he was a child. That childless woman had showered all her love on him, but that did not prevent her from occasionally giving expression to her strength of character. She had cracked more umbrellas over his head than his father had.

George heard the first cock crows and glimpsed the slow clearing of the night. The dogs were no longer barking, as they had the night before. Now the only sounds were the flight and chatter of small birds at the start of their busy day.

While George listened and ruminated, Heloise turned over lightly on her side and her foot brushed against George's knee. He ran a finger over her shoulder, and she complied by pressing her foot against his knee again. Then she smiled in her sleep.

George heard the voices of the family downstairs as they began to waken. He caressed Heloise, and then he too got up. He slipped on his djellaba, went out of the room, and slowly walked down the stairs. He kissed his hostess on both cheeks and sat down at the table, where everyone was eating steaming cornmeal and milk. Heloise soon joined them with her calm smile. The children stopped eating and eyed her curiously from behind their cups. The sound of a jeep came from the yard outside. George got up and went to the window. He waved hello and then turned and said, "Heloise, it's Tom. Remember? The guy who lent us the jeep."

The jeep stopped outside, and George went to open

the door. The merchant told George to invite his friends in, and so in came Tom, Amundsen, Nobel, and Ryland, single file with caps in hand.

"Hello," said George.

"Hello," Tom answered.

"What are you doing in this neck of the woods?" George asked.

"We were looking for you."

"Trouble?"

"A bit."

"What's it got to do with me?"

"Did you know you died?"

"Who? Me?"

"Three weeks ago."

"I died three weeks ago?"

"Yes."

"But that's not true!"

"Yes it is!"

"Where?"

"In goddam Lebanon."

"I died in goddam Lebanon?"

George was very much concerned with truth. The usual term is pragmatic. George was pragmatic.

At that moment little Ryland, who had been silent all the while, spoke up: "Private Smith, Margitai is trying to tell you that you were reported dead. Why, I do not know, since I can see that you are alive and well. Maybe it's because you didn't report to headquarters for several weeks. I think you are going to have to account for that omission. Where have you been all this time?"

"Around," George answered.

"Do you realize what you are saying?" Ryland asked.

"I think so. It means that you think I'm a deserter."

"You said it, not me."

"We found your body in a hole in open country," Amundsen said, and Nobel nodded in vigorous agreement.

"It wasn't a pretty sight," Amundsen went on, while Nobel continued to nod.

"It must have been someone else," said George.

"No doubt about it," Ryland concluded. And then he added: "Private George Smith, everything you say from this moment on may be used against you. You can name your own defense attorney, provided he is accredited in the United States of America."

"You mean I'm under arrest?"

"I guess so."

"Do I have to go with you?"

"Seems so."

"Heloise!" George thundered.

"Yes," she replied.

"We have to go."

"I'm ready."

George turned to his merchant friend, who had not understood very much of what he had heard. George embraced him, patted the man's wife on her cheek, and knelt down to say good-bye to the children. The old grandfather kept on eating, unaware of anything else going on. George said, "So long, Gramps."

"Bye," the old man replied, and he waved his hand without lifting his eyes from his bowl.

Then they all went outside. The two jeeps were parked one behind the other. Tom took the key from George and got behind the wheel of the one in front, with George and Amundsen behind him. Heloise got into the jeep being driven by Nobel. Ryland was the last to get in. The little clearing seemed deserted, and two hens slowly strutted in the motionless dust. The engines started up without much noise, and the vehicles started to move. The merchant and his wife stood for a long time in front of the door.

END OF CHAPTER NINE

INTERMEZZO
BETWEEN CHAPTERS
NINE AND TEN

Dear Abelard,

It occurs to me that aside from telling you how
Harry's Bar in Venice came into being, in all this time I
have never really talked to you about my father. So here
goes. One hot August evening in 1931, a few months
after opening Harry's Bar, he took my mother dancing at
the only place they knew at the time, the famous Martini
dance hall, owned and operated by Cavalier Baldi.

As far as alcoholic beverages are concerned, my father was probably the greatest barman of his era, and so
he remained for a great many years, partly because he
was mad about the drinks he mixed with such incredible bravura. If it had been up to him, he would often
have drunk a great deal, but what saved him from alco-
holism was the terrible hangover he usually had the
morning after a real bender. I could give you a detailed
account of all the sensations and the numerous and
frightening discomforts, because I too, to my good for-

tune and for reasons I will explain later, have suffered hangovers all my life, despite trying all kinds of ways to avoid them.

Whenever it happens—and it still does on occasion—that I lay my head down on the pillow because the room has no intention of staying still, it is as sure a thing as the national debt that about five o'clock the following morning I will wake from a gasping half-sleep in a state near death, a state marked by extensive hot and cold sweats and a murderous headache that throbs at every unusually rapid beat of my heart. The heartbeat intensifies the headache in geometric progression, and the only thing the heart seems to be doing is pumping a poisonous liquid that has nothing whatever to do with blood through veins and arteries.

Breathing is extremely rapid, and inhaling and exhaling are uncontrollable. The general impression is what any mortal must feel when he has only a few minutes left to balance his accounts before meeting his Maker. At this point the mere thought of imbibing even the smallest amount of alcohol is clearly unbearable torture. And the different sensations that usually go with this *post-bibendum* state are enough to make anyone a strict teetotaler for the rest of his presumably very short life. And then there's the added fact that because of business neither my father nor I have ever been able to enjoy a Sunday off, which, people say, is a great way to recover from the effects of liquor. Quite the contrary, even in the worst throes of this unbearable agony we have always had to get out of bed and carefully tread our way to work. Treading carefully is exactly what I mean, because it is hard to take more than thirty or forty steps without having to throw up, so you have to plan your itinerary in such a way that you can find some place that offers discreet protection from the eyes of perfidious busybodies.

Despite all the experience that ought to remind you of the disadvantages rather than the pleasures of wine and its derivatives, there often comes a moment in which you are overwhelmed by the innocent charm, freshness, and incomparable delight of good liquor. So, every now and again, in the evening, when all the customers in your bar have wined and dined, you set out a glass for yourself. You have no desire at all to set your head spinning, but you succumb to the pleasures of taste and smell. You are also in rather a hurry to close the place up after the last customer has paid his bill, and then you realize that you drank too fast, and you notice the first troubles the moment you get to your feet. These include difficulty in pronouncing correctly any word in which a nasal sound comes immediately after a sibilant, and you can't pronounce labials that aren't interspersed with a friendly vowel without twisting your tongue or getting it stuck against your palate. Words like Hasdrubal, for example, become all but unutterable. This is the point when you are torn between embarrassment that your inebriation may be discovered and a desire to proclaim forcefully all sorts of absurdities that strike you as truth.

You walk out of the place with an orderly lurch after a very affectionate leave-taking from your colleagues, whom at that moment you feel you love more than anyone else in the world. You are usually brought back to the real world when you run into a customer on the little steamer that takes you back home. You realize that if your condition is recognized, the report of the owner of Harry's Bar in a state of inebriation will go round the world faster than the speed of sound. So you try to hold yourself steady on the unsteady deck, and you still have to make intelligent responses to the idiotic remarks that usually come from the kind of people you casually encounter on shipboard. All this, of course, while you are doing everything you can to avoid words that might sound like Hasdrubal.

As you walk down the ramp, you make every effort to keep your eye on the ground in order not to stumble, and you walk very carefully so that no reeling motions betray your rather suspect condition. When you have finally gone around the first corner, you are all but indifferent to the fear of being seen from a window, and you let yourself go. You stagger so that you bounce from one wall to the other of the narrow *calle* leading home.

When you get to your door, there is a struggle to find the right key and somehow get it into the invisible lock. Once inside the darkness of your own home, you try not to make any sound that might awaken wife and children, for they would immediately recognize your shameful condition. A friend of mine was telling me about the terrible problems he has every time he comes home drunk late at night. He insists on taking a very large guitar with him, and his problem is to keep from banging it against the door frames and the furniture on his way to the double bed that is already half-occupied by his wife.

This is where I ought to explain why I have suffered all my life from the same aftereffects as my father. I think the trouble started right after my father and mother went home from Martini's that famous night in Venice. Young as they were, they followed certain procedures that resulted in my conception. Since my father had bent his elbow considerably that evening, they worried for a long time whether the fruit of their union might come into this world with some mysterious affliction. But this was not the case, except for an endless string of trivial ailments that afflicted me throughout childhood and made my skin so pale that every now and then my father would ask if a fart had got into my bloodstream. I did have a mysterious ailment after all, and my father probably suffered from it for the same hereditary reason I did: it seems that my late grandfather Carlo had the habit, as people did in his day, of drowning in wine the joys and sorrows that usually accompany our life on earth.

END OF THE INTERMEZZO
BETWEEN CHAPTERS
NINE AND TEN

CHAPTER TEN

In which George and Heloise are taken to the headquarters of the armed forces of the United States of America.

One jeep followed the other over the dirt road. George was in the second jeep and could see nothing in front of him except a great deal of thick white dust. Finally they reached the barrier of the Israeli-controlled zone, and from that point on the road was asphalt. Now George caught an occasional glimpse of Heloise's windblown hair. He felt a bit depressed and utterly unable to guess what might happen.

They all got out at headquarters. Heloise turned to George. She gave him a tender smile, and he felt better at once. Together they went up to General Custer's anteroom. Two MPs were standing at attention outside the door, their helmets down to their eyes. Ryland went up to them. "I'm Lieutenant Ryland with Sergeants Amundsen and Nobel, Privates Margitai, and Smith, and"—Ryland cleared his throat as he looked at Heloise—"this lady. We have to see the general."

One of the MPs did an about-face and knocked on the general's door.

Suzy's answer came like a shout: "Yes?"

"Lieutenant Ryland requests permission to speak with the general."

"Come in." Custer's voice came through peremptorily.

They all went in.

"Lieutenant Ryland reporting, sir." He snapped to attention.

"Make it quick, Ryland. So you're Private Smith," the general said.

"I am, sir," George said.

"Well, well, well, well, so you're Smith?"

"Yes sir, General."

"Hm, Smith?"

"Yes sir, General."

General Custer seemed to be having trouble formulating his next question. "Well, well, well, well," he repeated himself, "and how are you?"

"Very well, sir."

"Well, well, well, well."

Custer had caught sight of Heloise in the meantime, and as he continued to repeat "well, well," he seemed unable to take his eyes off her. It was very much like what had happened the first time he saw Suzy in his office.

Ryland spoke. "I've already explained his responsibilities to him, and I told him to get legal counsel, sir."

"What?" Custer exclaimed. "You asked him to get a lawyer?"

"Yes sir, General."

"Ryland," Custer thundered. "What ever gave you such an idea. Where did you get the authority to say something like that? What were my orders to you? Margitai!"

"Yes sir."

"What were my orders?"

"To find Private Smith, this lady, and my jeep."

"And did you?"

"Yes sir, General."

"Fine! Did I ask you to do anything else?"

"No sir."

"Right! Is that right, Ryland?"

"Well."

"Well what? Yes or no?"

"Yes sir, General."

"Ryland, you think too much. You mustn't think, because you don't know how to think. Let others do the thinking for you! Always! Understand?"

"Yes sir," Ryland mumbled. He was depressed.

"And now get out of here." He nodded at Amundsen, Nobel, and Ryland.

Custer, Tom, George, Heloise, and Suzy were alone now.

Custer got up from his chair, walked around the desk, and put both hands on Smith's shoulders. "Dear boy, we are proud of you."

George was rather embarrassed, but he managed to get out the words "Thank you, sir."

"I know all about it, all about it," Custer said. "They must have been four terrible weeks. Did you suffer a great deal? How did they treat you?"

George did not understand what the general was driving at, but he thought it better to go along with him and answered, "Well, it could have been worse, sir."

"Such modesty! It must have been sheer hell, being

a prisoner of those bandits. And you, ma'am?" He turned to Heloise but didn't wait for an answer. Then he turned to Tom. "Margitai! Thank you for rescuing Private George Smith. Thank you in the name of the United States Army. I am going to recommend you for a medal."

"Thank you, sir." Tom smiled.

"Now get those jeeps back to the motor pool," the general ordered.

"Yes sir."

"And another thing, Margitai!"

"Yes sir."

"Don't lose them!" The general smiled.

"No chance, sir."

"Well, well, well, well," Custer said, sinking contentedly against the back of his chair. Meanwhile Heloise had taken the chair Suzy offered her.

"Where did they capture you?" Custer asked George.

"Hm, outside Harry's Bar."

"What impudence!" the general exclaimed. "And where did they take you?"

"To a village."

"Ah!"

"We had nothing to eat or drink for four days," said George, playing along.

"Swine!" said Custer as he brought his fist down on the table.

"Then we managed to escape," George said. "This lady and myself."

"Well, well, well, well," Custer said.

"They chased us across the desert for days and days."

"You don't say?"

"It was rough," George said, "but we saved the jeep."

"Well done!"

"And today we found Margitai and the others."

"Is there anything you need?"

"I'd like to let my aunt in Alabama know I'm OK."

"Already done," Custer said.

"Thank you, sir."

"I have also faxed the President. He is looking forward to seeing you in Washington and congratulating you himself—and he wants to give you the Medal of Honor personally."

"I don't deserve it," George said.

"That's up to us to decide," said Custer, cutting him short. And then he added: "I suggest we go out and celebrate. What do you say?"

"It sounds great to me," said Suzy.

"Let's go to Harry's Bar," Custer said as he stood up.

They all went out, Suzy leading the way, then Heloise, and finally Custer and George. Custer put his arm around George's shoulder, while his eyes were drawn irresistibly to Heloise's quivering gluteals, as she walked ahead of him aquiver as usual and slightly unsteady on her dusty, high-heeled, black patent leather evening shoes.

END OF CHAPTER TEN

INTERMEZZO
BETWEEN CHAPTERS
TEN AND ELEVEN

Dear Abelard,

I have already mentioned the grim castle in Somerset where my father sent me one winter in the early 1950s to study English, a language you almost have to know in my business.

The owner of this castle was a mild-mannered, very British-looking gentleman, one of those people they use in television advertisements for Scotch whisky. His salient features were a ruddy complexion, a set of whiskers that grew right up to his eyes, and two buckteeth, the kind people sometimes end up with if they were thumbsuckers as babies.

His helpmate was about twenty years younger than he, a little brunette who wasn't half bad. There was an odd, intermittent gasp in her laugh that might have been quite appropriate in certain interesting situations.

There was also a cook. Her distinguishing feature was her missing denture and her boundless love for the song "You Belong to Me," which she was forever playing on a little phonograph in the kitchen. She was very good at enriching Campbell's soups with a few drops of cream. She too was caught up in the lively atmosphere of the manor and busied herself at night by giving dazzling parties in her room, to which she invited the stableboys and the men and women servants of the house.

The dining room had three walls of austere walnut wainscot, and the fourth wall consisted of a magnificent window overlooking the grounds. The dining-room table was dominated by a huge cylindrical cactus, from which two enormous red glasses dangled on a red ribbon. The phallic reference was clear to everyone.

That is where I idled away three short months one bitter-cold English winter. Occasionally a letter would come from my father. He had only gone to sixth grade in Germany before the First World War, but when it came to sending stern yet loving instructions, he wrote simple, extremely effective prose. To tell the truth, I did not receive very many of these missives in my time, because I was more obedient than reprobate as a son; but when they came, they always filled me with heavy yet salutary feelings of guilt.

After receiving one of these letters, I decided to move to London, where I lived the first three days on the proceeds of twelve country-fresh eggs that I had brought from Somerset and sold to a buxom waitress. In London I shared a room with a Swedish girl, which is the main reason why I still have a strange accent when I speak English.

At that time my future career had still not been settled for me, though I already had my suspicions. Until I was nineteen, I had always considered my name a simple family oddity. My father had opened Harry's Bar in Venice for business about a year before my mother brought me into the world. Both of them thought it was perfectly normal to call me Arrigo, even though I had no grandfathers or great-grandfathers of that name, and there had never been even a trace of an Arrigo anywhere in the family.

The English for Arrigo is Harry, and though it is perfectly ordinary for a bar to be named for a barman, it is quite exceptional that a boy be named for a bar. The fact that I was the only person in the world who had been named after a bar should at least have made me suspicious.

I finished high school in 1949, and we discussed as a family what I would do in the future. Discussed in a manner of speaking, because very little attention was paid to my opinions in these family gatherings. Personally I would have liked to become a race-car driver, but there was absolutely no place for that sort of thing in either of the only two broad categories my father would allow: study or work.

It was decided without further ado that I would study law at the University of Padua, partly because there was a law office over Harry's Bar where I could work as a legal apprentice. I think the vicinity of the bar had some influence on my father's decision. After all, he probably thought, if that doesn't pan out, he can always come downstairs and work.

My life in those years is a dream that I have happily cherished all these years.

In our free time, and there was a lot of it in Padua, we played billiards. We went to the retired officers' mess for lunch, not just because it was inexpensive, 150 lire, but mainly to try to date a couple of very blond waitresses who were the sole ornaments of that austere place. We were not concerned with the great social issues. Our leader, Tribuno, was a third-year medical student who sat himself down in the anatomy professor's chair at the beginning of the first lecture of the academic year. When we had elections at school we used punches and shoves instead of votes to support our candidates. I don't know if that was right or wrong, but it was certainly more congenial to the modest political capabilities of our brains. In the evening I usually dragged my drowsy twenty-year-old self to Harry's Bar so my father could take a break. And that was how things went until exam time, without a care in the world.

The Foundations of Private Law was the first reef I encountered in law school. It was there that my legal career actually came to an end. I barely passed the exam. That was at three in the afternoon. At six o'clock I walked down the stairs from the law office and got up on the stool behind the cash register in Harry's Bar.

END OF THE INTERMEZZO
BETWEEN CHAPTERS
TEN AND ELEVEN

CHAPTER ELEVEN

In which Harry Cipriani wakes up on the wrong side of the bed and begins a new day.

Many historians have gone to a great deal of trouble to recount the deeds of the Prince of Condé. One of the best-known details is how incredibly calm he was the night before the battle of Rocroi. The Great Condé slept soundly through the night without a moment's interruption. His admirers, however, have gone to any length to foster a cult of personality, and they have almost always glossed over certain details that might actually have been extremely important. No one, for example, has ever told us what the prince ate for dinner that night before he went to bed. There is no way of knowing now, but it seems doubtful that our hero had much more than a steak and a salad. If, for example, his orderly had arranged for the cook to prepare spareribs and sauerkraut, there is no doubt that the Spaniards would have fared better in the battle, and history might have taken an altogether different course.

Harry Cipriani, the owner of Harry's Bar in Beirut,

woke up about four in the morning. He was covered in perspiration and breathing heavily. A horrible dream had been tormenting him for an hour. The main character in his nightmare was Raspetti, the awful food critic who was the darling of the upwardly mobile classes.

Harry's dream was that the *Times'* Bryan Miller was having dinner and shouting across the room as he waved an enormous cockroach he said he found in his fish soup. Raspetti and four *Michelin Guide* inspectors were at the next table, and when they saw what was happening they burst out laughing. Several customers got up and walked out in disgust. And Harry, immobilized by shame, was stammering meaningless phrases.

Fortunately, he woke up at that point. His pasty mouth immediately reminded him of the previous night's menu: beef stew and lyonnaise potatoes. And the bottle and a half of cabernet he had drunk was still gurgling in his stomach. He got up for a drink of water and to slow his heartbeat. His heart continued to pound even after he woke up from the nightmare.

He couldn't get back to sleep, so at six o'clock he went out for the morning papers. By seven o'clock he had already downed five cups of coffee and was beginning to feel better, but he knew his day was ruined. He waited until the cleaning people came at seven-thirty and then began to go over the previous day's receipts. Business was good. The Beirut bar was probably the most profitable after the ones in Venice and New York. The odd war that had been going on for years brought a great many people to Beirut—newspapermen, curiosity seekers, gunrunners, and a host of tourists as well. They crossed the Atlantic on War-Express charter flights for the excitement of experiencing a bombing.

The main thrill of the tour was that you could buy the return ticket only in Beirut a few minutes before the return flight. There was deathly suspense in the air until the very last moment. And this last-ditch atmosphere substantially increased people's willingness to spend. People who had money were happy to spend it all—who knows, they might die at any moment. People who didn't have any money cheerfully used up all their credit on the assumption that death would cancel all debts. So the cash register rang and the IOUs mounted rapidly at Harry's Bar. Harry was not too worried about the IOUs: his sister Karmel was a fine lawyer, and her specialty was bad-debt collection.

The doors of Harry's Bar opened about ten o'clock in the morning. There were several different phases of a day at Harry's. Kitchen activity was the main thing in the morning. The dining room was often empty then, and it was normal to hear the sounds of pots and pans and the rapid remarks the cooks exchanged as they got things ready for the day. A customer wandered in from time to time. At that hour they usually ordered coffee or orange juice.

About eleven o'clock that particular morning—and it wasn't the first time—a tour leader opened both doors to show the dining room to a couple of dozen men and women who were visiting sanctuaries of all the religions. Harry's Bar was one of them. More than once Harry had thought of installing a holy-wine fount by the door so that these pilgrims could dip their fingers and make the sign of the cross.

The regular customers usually turned up at eleven-thirty; they were the ones who boasted that they had attended the opening eight years before. A table was set aside for them every day. Harry referred to them as the senators. They were not people whose presence attracted attention, but you noticed at once if they weren't there. As the day went on, the small room, fifteen by thirty feet in all, began to take on a life of its own. This may have been the inmost secret of Harry's Bar. It was the human spirit that dominated the place, but within the boundaries Harry laid down. They were the boundaries of civility, which had been passed down to Harry by his father, who had learned them from his grandfather, who in turn had tried to grasp everything his great-grandfather taught him.

Waves of feeling constantly rolled across the room and met without colliding, because they arose from the heart of what was best in people. Harry perceived the leitmotiv of this equilibrium as the enduring sound of a balanced and well-tempered harmony.

If anyone or anything upset this harmony, Harry intervened at once. It wasn't always easy, but things always got straightened out in the end. The life force came from everywhere: from the kitchen, where the cooks were under constant pressure; from the bar, where the waiters were attentive but relaxed in serving the customers; and from the reassuring presence of Harry himself, who shared their life from morning to night.

That day, there was still almost no one there at noon, when General Custer walked into the bar with George, Heloise, and Suzy.

As usual Harry had accepted far more reservations than there were tables. He always did. Not for lucre, but just because he hated to say no. He found it an intolerable discourtesy to refuse someone a table.

The general walked in first, and Harry greeted him with the blend of natural courtesy and affection he would have shown a relative.

"Harry, have you got a table?" Custer asked.

"Take this one." Harry led him to the left corner table, the best table in the house. Harry had already promised it to three different parties that morning on the telephone.

"Hello, Private Smith." Harry turned to Heloise. "Hello, madam. And how are you?" he asked Suzy. Without another word Harry brought them four Bellinis. This was the time of the year, August, when the peaches had a marvelous pink color and the Bellini was at its peak.

Whether it was thirst, the refreshing cool taste of the drink, or the very delicate fruit flavor that sweetly attenuated the tartness of the champagne, the fact remains that anyone with an unencumbered soul would have drunk Bellinis by the dozen.

A few minutes later other people began to arrive. Some of them were important people, and some of them were less important, but they all had one purpose in mind: to go to Harry's Bar and see Harry. The level of background noise gradually increased, but it was never unbearable, and you could always hear your companions, even when speaking softly.

Almost the only thing the general talked about was the drinks and Harry.

After half an hour, Suzy got up. "Shall we powder our noses?" she asked Heloise.

As soon as the two men were alone, Custer turned to George. "You goddam son of a bitch, where the hell were you?"

"Uh," replied George, "with her," and he nodded at Heloise's vacant chair.

"But where?" Custer exclaimed.

"In a hotel," George lied.

"In a goddam hotel! You spent two weeks in a goddam hotel," Custer asked, "without even leaving the goddam room?"

"Yes."

"With her?" This time Custer nodded at Heloise's chair.

"Yes, sir."

"For the glory and freedom of the United States of America! That's the first time I've heard that one in all these years. In a hotel room for two weeks! Did you, by any chance, lose the key?"

"Uh, well, I didn't remember where I'd put it." George smiled.

"Listen," Custer said, "before the ladies come back, I've got something to say to you. It will be a lot better for you if this business remains a totally personal goddam fact between us. I mean between you, me, and that goddam Ryland. It will be much better for you, for me, for goddam Ryland, and for the United States of America! Got that?"

"Yes sir, General."

"And stop saying 'General' all the time. You can call me the stupid general in command of the stupidest division of the great US Army!" Custer spoke in a low voice, but his words came out knife sharp in short bursts, and his face got redder and redder.

The two women reappeared in the doorway across the room. Custer gave George a hearty pat on the back and exclaimed, "I'm delighted to be here with our hero!

Harry, four more Bellinis! Hi there, Arafat!" He waved at Arafat Jr., who was sitting two tables away.

Harry brought a tablecloth with the Bellinis and spread it out before them. "The kidney is marvelous today, General. You might like them sliced and sautéed, and maybe some green asparagus with oil and vinegar."

"That sounds great, Harry," Custer said. He turned to the others. "And you?"

"That would be fine," said Heloise.

"Me too," said Suzy.

"And George just loves kidneys, don't you, George?" Custer asked.

"Yes sir."

"All right, Harry, kidney for four and a bottle of cabernet, your stock, please."

"Very well, General," Harry said and finished setting the table.

END OF CHAPTER ELEVEN

INTERMEZZO
BETWEEN CHAPTERS
ELEVEN AND TWELVE

Dear Abelard,

I wouldn't want you to misunderstand what I said the other day, that if Heloise had insisted on paying her share of the bill the first time they went to Harry's Bar, she and George would never have had a love affair. The reason you do not understand me is that you are always determined at any cost to play the protector of the oppressed and exploited. As if the immanent order of things assigned women to that category. I am just trying to open your eyes.

What I am trying to tell you is this: Remember the other day, when you were looking under your girl-friend's skirt to check the bodywork on her contraption, and with the most innocent air in the world she asked you to lend her three million lire? At that moment, when things couldn't have been more delightful, the woman who is now your ex-fiancée was simply asking what she considered her due after all this time. I.e., you cannot expect to be offered the use of her contraption for fifteen years without once giving the owner the slightest hope of one day walking her down the aisle. What's more, you were too insensitive at the time to notice that she tactfully asked you for a loan, not a gift. I am talking about the three million lire. A loan that she obviously would have been willing to repay you after the wedding, so to speak. You are always criticizing me and setting yourself up as the defender of the weak, but you want everything, and gratis, to boot. You are the real exploiter of women. You can hardly wait to call her a whore, when all she wanted was what you owed her.

Sure, three million lire might seem too much for once around the block, but it is almost nothing when you think of all the times she has let you have a good look in all these years. Let me give you some practical advice in case you should be in that sort of situation again. And I have no doubt that you will, since you are so congenitally cheap. There are proven methods for getting out of situations like that. At least temporarily.

Instead of dropping everything and slamming the door behind you, which is what you did (without even finishing what you were up to, by the way, which I would have thought the best thing to do at the time), you might at least have stalled for time. You could have said that you had to go through your accountant to make that kind of loan. You would have made a marvelous impression, and she wouldn't have known you don't have three million lire to your name or, for that matter, that you've never even seen three million lire at one time. So, when you're in that situation again, remember the accountant dodge. That's what really rich people do. They never have money on them. All their money is in the company. They almost never have liquid assets. (Anyone with a million lire in his pocket must surely be just over the poverty line.) Even though you wouldn't pass for being really rich, you could carry a checkbook—but of course it's the company account, and you can't use that either without bona fide receipts.

I remember a famous lawyer from Turin who came to Harry's Bar in Venice for lunch one day. Everyone thought he must be extremely rich, but actually all he had at his personal disposal was a small amount every now and then. After lunching with a lady, he got up from the table and took a handkerchief and a hundred-dollar bill from his pocket. He gave the waiter the hundred dollars and walked out of the place, and everyone wondered whether the hundred dollars was meant to pay for lunch or if it was a tip for the waiter.

Of course nobody dared to ask him. The tab was more than a hundred dollars—our prices are rather high, as you know. So the waiter kept his hundred-dollar tip, and that tab still sits among pending bills that will never be paid.

I have another friend who used to slip a neatly folded hundred-dollar bill between the thigh and garter belt of a very close friend every time she let him use her contraption. One day, after many years, this friend did not have the usual hundred-dollar bill, so he slipped a hundred-thousand-lire note between her thigh and garter belt. He had checked the exchange rate that morning on the financial page, and the note was worth exactly one hundred dollars.

His girlfriend couldn't have been more offended. The way my friend and I explained it was that lire were considered as payment, while dollars were a gift. It's as if to say that if this friend of mine and his girlfriend had been in America, it would have been perfectly logical for him to slip a hundred-thousand-lire note between her thigh and garter belt, but it would have been quite improper to use dollars in that situation.

Let me give you some advice. Wherever you are in the world, make sure you always have a certain amount of currency from another country. It will come in handy as a welcome gift on any occasion.

END OF THE INTERMEZZO
BETWEEN CHAPTERS
ELEVEN AND TWELVE

CHAPTER TWELVE

*In which General Custer is rather drunk by the
end of lunch at Harry's Bar.*

Meanwhile, an American couple in their fifties sat
down at the next table. He was wearing a blue Lacoste
shirt and loud tartan trousers and had a heavy gold
bracelet on his wrist. Her Kewpie-doll face was hidden
under a very broad-brimmed white hat.

The man smiled at Harry and asked, "Where's
Harry?"

"I'm Harry," Harry replied.

Harry's face remained expressionless, and that
made the man laugh all the harder. "Oh," he said,
"that's all right, I believe you."

"What can I get you?" Harry asked. "Would you like
a Bellini?"

"What's a Bellini?"

"Peach nectar and champagne."

"Champagne? Champagne of course. Yes, that's
fine, and what'll you have?"

"Make mine a Bellini too," his wife said.

Harry went to the counter and asked Ruggero, the barman, for two Bellinis. Then he looked toward the door, where Kissinger's son had just walked in with Jim Kennedy. Young Kissinger shook his hand, and then the two customers went over and sat down at Arafat Jr.'s table. Arafat got up to greet them. "I'm expecting young Gorbachev."

"Cipriani!" the elderly Countess Venier called from her table.

"Yes, Countess."

"Don't forget the tickets for the Red Cross concert!"

"Yes, Countess."

"And the roses for the Crusaders' party!"

"Yes, Countess."

"How many would you like this year?"

"How much do they cost?"

"I don't know yet."

"In that case, none." Harry smiled.

"No! You have to!"

Countess Venier raised her imperious chin and pursed her narrow lips. She didn't know whether to laugh or be angry. She often failed to understand Harry's humor.

"A hundred. Will that do?"

"Good! I'll send them over on August twenty-fifth. What time do you want them?"

"About ten."

Meanwhile, Countess Venier had been joined by Countess Maecenas, who had been quite arteriosclerotic for some years.

"Cipriani!" Countess Maecenas said. "I was here the day you opened."

"Yes, Countess."

"My friends came to get me in a coach at the villa. 'There's a little bar in town,' they said. 'Why don't you come along to the cocktail party they're giving for the opening?' And so I did."

"I was there too," said Countess Venier.

"I don't think you were," said Countess Maecenas, shrugging her shoulders. Countess Venier gave Countess Maecenas a compassionate look but said nothing.

"Cipriani!" Countess Maecenas called out again, as she rummaged feverishly through her oversize bag.

"Yes, Countess."

"Lend me fifty dollars. I can't find my wallet."

"Yes, Countess," Harry sighed. This would be the third time in four days that he had lent the countess fifty dollars. He would never see the money again, because she completely forgot about each loan as soon as she received it.

He went to the desk and asked for fifty dollars and then returned to her table. The countess was waiting for him with her wallet open.

"Look what's inside," Harry said.

"Well, I've got a hundred dollars," replied Countess Maecenas.

"That's what I gave you yesterday and the day before," said Harry.

"That's not possible!" she said. "I just got that from the administrator for the rent."

"All right, Countess," Harry sighed. "But then you don't need anything now."

"I really don't understand." Countess Maecenas turned to Countess Venier, who was not listening. "After all these years. I was his first customer. And now he won't give me fifty dollars. Cipriani!"

"Yes, Countess."

"Bring me a *Rabarbaro!*"

"At once, madam."

"I'll have one too," said Countess Venier.

"Very well, Countess."

That's how it was. Every day. Old Mr. Quolter was there too, sitting in the corner with his wife. As usual, after the fourth martini his drawn-out, gasping, life-threatening cough started up, and his face turned an alarming shade of purple. Two waiters lifted him under the armpits and carried him outside while his legs pedaled the air and a sound like a death rattle came from under his blondish mustache.

"He's slipping away!" Colonel Cervi solemnly remarked from his corner.

Harry had difficulty suppressing a smile.

"Cipriani!" shouted Countess Maecenas, who had noticed nothing.

"Yes, Countess."

"Would you lend me fifty dollars. I forgot my wallet."

That is how the day was progressing at Harry's Bar.

The senators were having a lively discussion at their table about the letter *F* in the encyclopedia. The Concorde flight engineer was explaining how he managed to get from Ancona to Palermo by way of Tel Aviv, but no one paid much attention to him. Sitting in the middle, Earl Gillam was the only one to smile at the tale of the Concorde engineer's adventures. Everyone else seemed quite bored. Gillam's brother Victor had died at the age of eighty-three, sitting at a table in Renato's bar in the Carpathians. He just leaned forward and put his forehead in a plate of steaming spaghetti. He was a sturdy fellow and extremely intelligent. He took life as it came, without ever trying to change the way things were.

Custer and his guests were having ice cream. They had already finished four bottles of cabernet. Custer rambled as he spoke. "This George, you know, madam, he is truly a real hero. A very great hero. And that's because he's nice too. Because, if he wasn't such a nice guy, he'd be just another son of a . . . woman I know. But he's not. George is a hero. And foxy. He knocked everybody for a loop with his foxiness. His enemies, his friends, the army, and, if you'll pardon me, you too maybe. Do you know that you are a remarkable woman? Suzy! Heloise is remarkable! Don't you think so? Any man could be a hero for a woman like that."

George, Heloise, and Suzy all smiled in amusement.

"General," Suzy said, "it's going to be a long war, and it's time to get some sleep." Suzy nodded at Harry for the bill, which, as usual, was to be sent to headquarters.

"George!" Custer thundered.

"Yes sir, General."

"America is proud of both of you!"

"I'm Czech," Heloise murmured.

"Czechoslovakia is proud too! And you are a truly beautiful woman!"

"General, we ought to be going now," Suzy prodded. "We have to watch maneuvers tomorrow."

"Suzy is right, we ought to go." Custer got up and suddenly felt dizzy. He stood still for a moment until he regained his sense of balance.

"And where are you two going?" he asked George.

"We're going upstairs to rest," George replied.

"Free pass this evening!" Custer exclaimed.

"You'll have to come to the base tomorrow," Suzy said. "We have to make plans for the trip." She took Custer by the arm and helped him toward the check-room.

A minute later Custer was sitting next to Suzy in the jeep, as George and Heloise watched from the doorway of Harry's Bar. Suzy put the vehicle in gear, and Custer waved them a feeble good-bye without looking in their direction. All his energy seemed suddenly to have gone out of him. The jeep moved off smoothly in the hot afternoon sun.

Neither of them said a word as Suzy speeded down the uncrowded streets. It was ten minutes before they got to her place. Custer dropped onto the sofa. "Son of a bitch. That big son of a bitch," he sighed wearily. Then he fell asleep, his head drooping to one side. Suzy lifted his legs firmly but delicately onto the sofa, took off his shoes, and then tiptoed out to the garden.

END OF CHAPTER TWELVE

INTERMEZZO
BETWEEN CHAPTERS
TWELVE AND THIRTEEN

Dear Abelard,

The two customers at the table next to our heroes' were nosy Americans, nosy as only Americans can be— which is not to say that customers from other countries aren't just as nosy about what goes on in a bar or restaurant.

Some customers ask you about the history of the place, and they are in the majority. Others want to know how much money you take in, how many meals you serve in a day, how big a staff you have, how old the owner is; and where did Hemingway and Orson Welles sit, how many husbands did Barbara Hutton have, and a lot of other absolutely meaningless things.

I would have been very happy to be the latest in a long line of saloonkeepers: after all, a dynasty is always a dynasty. And, if nothing else, it would be very nice to have your brain furnished at birth with ideas that got there, so to speak, by heredity. But the history of my forebears doesn't go much farther back than the pedigree of an Ethiopian slave sold cheap in Alabama.

My paternal grandfather, that is to say, my father's father, was the late Carlo, whom I've already mentioned. As you know, Italy, like all countries with a high standard of living, has always been very concerned about the psychological and physical well-being of minorities. Getting the father's name off public documents was one of our young democracy's first frontline battles. Everyone was justifiably worried about the possible psychic trauma of people who had never met their male parent and were obliged to publicize the fact by writing the incriminating letters "F.U." I have never been able to decide if "father unknown" is most demeaning to the father, the mother, or the innocent child born of the union of two careless people.

I am not sure that this victory of democracy was altogether a good thing. I remember meeting old Angelo Rizzoli, the famous publisher. I read somewhere that he was a foundling, but he certainly showed no signs of the wound that should have been inflicted by never having known his parents.

The reason for telling you all this is to explain that it is just because of my father's papers that I learned I was the grandson of the late Carlo. I don't know what my grandmother's name was, partly because the mother's name was always optional in official documents. I knew her only from what my father said. He always referred to her as "my poor mother"; and he always referred to his father as "my poor father." As a boy, I thought that "poor" just meant that they were dead. When I was older, I understood that the adjective was applied to summarize two distinct features of my forebears: that they were deceased, yes, but that they had died in the same state of extreme poverty in which they had always lived. My father's late father was also miserably lacking in wherewithal.

There are a lot of people who cannot use the terms "my poor mother" or "my poor father" in speaking of their late parents because when the deceased were alive they had such good fortune they could afford to turn their nose up at beans and get back to their mayonnaise.

One of the advantages of "father unknown" is that he never dies. There is no such thing as "deceased father unknown." He is No Name forever, much more present than any dearly departed. No Name is not necessarily a poor man. Quite the contrary, he may have been rich, rich and dissolute, astute and rarely unhappy. It is not all that uncommon for a No Name to become rich and spend the rest of his life tracking down the fruit of his sin. And there are those who have been deeply disappointed by their success in this pursuit. If we could turn back the clock, I would be in favor of giving the father's name in official documents. There is certainly no harm in official acknowledgment when the father is known. And if the father is unknown, freewheeling fantasies about the versatile personality of Mr. No Name can only stimulate the mind of the lucky offspring.

And another thing. How could you ever reconstruct a family history three hundred years from now, say, without some document to tell you who was the son of whom? Without documents, you'd have to rely on hearsay. Nowadays in official papers I am nobody's son; and my son is in the same situation, for that matter. So when I tell the history of Harry's Bar, people just have to take my word for things.

Let me tell you, everybody is very interested in the history of restaurants and bars. To tell the truth, I am convinced that Adam had a bar of his own, and everything ever written or told about the origin of the world is simply the story Adam used to tell his customers about how his bar got started.

If you remember, the two Americans in Beirut asked Harry who Harry was, but they didn't really believe him when he told them. The same thing happens to me in Venice. What's more, every time I tell someone how and why my father, Giuseppe, opened the bar in the first place, my intention is to clarify things for the person I am talking to, but I am fully aware that I am spreading what will one day be narrated as pure legend.

It goes more or less like this:

In the beginning was gin, whiskey, rum, and cognac. And these four things were never to be mixed together. Then came other things, such as vermouth, sweet liqueurs, sugar, and lemon, which were created to serve the greater glory of the first four elements of the world.

On the sixth day God created the Barman. Instead of Eve, He gave him a shaker, then ice, and then a couple of glasses. And He said: "Mix for the joy of your neighbors."

My father, Giuseppe, was born in Verona, the son of an immigrant, the late Carlo. In 1929 he was working as a barman at the Hotel Europa in Venice. One of his disciples was a young American named Harry. He was very rich but, to our great good fortune, he did not have an American Express credit card. It was one of the things that hadn't yet been invented.

If there had been credit cards in 1929, there would never have been a Harry's Bar.

I'll tell you why.

One day the rich young American named Harry suddenly stopped drinking at my father Giuseppe's counter. Listless and melancholy, he would wander among the tables in the tearoom, indifferent to the glances of those adorable creatures who usually made such pleasant company in tearooms and their environs. My father was a true gentleman, but he was also a practical man; and he never failed to register the mood of his customers and the amount of the day's receipts. After a while he went up to the young man and asked, "Mr. Pickering, you're not ill by any chance?"

"No, Mr. Cipriani," Pickering answered dejectedly.

"Maybe you don't like the way my drinks taste anymore?"

"Oh no, Mr. Cipriani."

"Found a bar you like better?"

"No, no, Mr. Cipriani."

"Well then, what's the matter?"

"Nothing, Mr. Cipriani." Mr. Pickering sounded sad and seemed to be hiding something he dare not confess.

"You're not broke?" my father asked him.

"Yes, Mr. Cipriani!"

"How much do you need?"

"Why, would you give me money?" Mr. Pickering could hardly believe it.

"It depends how much you need."

"Just enough to pay the hotel, the bar, go home, and have a last dry martini" was Harry Pickering's answer.

This is how that rather reckless young man with a nice honest face got a substantial loan from my father (not without my mother's approval, however). He repaid the loan two years later, and at the beginning he was also a partner in Harry's Bar in Venice, which was named after him.

You see, if Mr. Pickering had had a credit card, he could have used it to pay his bill. He would have gone his merry way and never have made that loan arrangement, which was the only real bargain my father ever struck in his long, brilliant, and hardworking career.

Actually, George Smith reminded my grandson Harry Cipriani of Harry Pickering, which is why my grandson extended his credit beyond any reasonable limit.

END OF THE INTERMEZZO
BETWEEN CHAPTERS
TWELVE AND THIRTEEN

CHAPTER THIRTEEN

*In which General Custer wakes in the night,
recites a poem, and reaches out to Suzy.*

Custer awakened suddenly at one in the morning. He
could not have said what it was that woke him up. It
might have been a distant rifle shot echoing through
the night or the end of a dream he couldn't figure out.

He thought Harry's wine must have been very
good, because the only aftereffect of all the drinking
the day before was a great thirst. It was an effort to get
up from the sofa, and he groped his way to the veranda
door. The pale light of night shone in, and the air felt
cool and smooth.

He stood looking at the still mirror of water in the
pool, which reflected the billions of bright pinpoints in
the galaxy. He leaned against the veranda door frame
and thought about George. Because of all the incredible
mess involved in finding Smith, Custer ought to have
hated the man, but he actually liked the son of a bitch;
indeed, he felt something he might well call affection.
Physically, George reminded him of his son in Amer-

ica, a law student, and Custer had always had an enormous weakness for the boy. There was something good yet strong about George that won over anyone who spent even half an hour with him. He had a smile that came straight from his eyes and then quickly spread over his face as he crinkled his lids. His eyes took on a sweet, innocent, and harmless expression that attracted everyone, men and women alike.

Then Custer's thoughts turned to Heloise. He found her an incredibly beautiful woman. That afternoon at lunch it had almost hurt. How much he wished he were young again. He tried to recall a poem he'd thought up when he was in Vietnam. He was driving a jeep at the time, when for no apparent reason the image of a friend's wife popped into his head and stayed there for a while.

> *How I wish that I could find*
> *A small room in your mind,*
> *Just a little place*
> *With your pretty face.*
>
> *How I wish that I could be*
> *The briefest melody*
> *In the calmness kind*
> *Of your lovely mind.*
>
> *How I wish that you could be*
> *One evening just for me,*
> *That your silent tread*
> *Brought you to my bed.*

The memory moved him, and he uttered a deep sigh. It was the alcohol that made him feel sorry for himself. He didn't care whether it was good for him or not. Thanks to Harry's wine and cocktails, he could experience anew some very beautiful past emotions. It was partly because he felt very young inside, much younger than Ryland, for example, who must have been at least twenty years his junior. Custer walked slowly back into the house and went to the kitchen for a glass of water. He turned out the light and went to Suzy's room without making a sound. The door was open, and some of the clearness of the night shone through the curtains. Suzy was sound asleep in a large double bed just like the one Custer had shared with all his women over the past ten years.

As always, he was fascinated by how quietly Suzy slept. He had often gone right up to her nose to feel her very regular breathing, to make sure she was alive.

He slipped into bed slowly and lay on his side, taking up very little room.

There were times when he felt weighed down by his responsibilities. He would have liked to be back home in America. He could see himself as a grandfather.

He would have let his grandchildren get away with anything, he was sure of that. But he would never let them go into the army. He hadn't let his son do so either. Custer himself had never felt that he was a real soldier. The good sense he had used so abundantly throughout his military career would have made him a success in any field. He had a gift for smoothing things out. It occurred to him that idiots were the raw material of his success, and he laughed at the thought. It was only thanks to idiots that he had become a general. Now he had to organize the triumphal return of George, though he was fully aware that everyone knew the truth, probably even the President. He also thought that nobody saw things the way he did, except for Suzy and a very few others. There weren't many people to whom he could say, "We talk the same language."

He had known a Japanese grand master of karate once, a man who always had a smile on his face. He would try to explain or demonstrate something that looked, and probably was, very simple, but for that very reason was extremely hard to do. And he would look at the people around him with an odd, questioning glance and ask if by any chance they didn't think he was right. He had an ungainly but very strong body and a sublime mind that had an incredibly childlike genuineness to it. Truly great men are like that. They marvel at nothing, because nothing can amaze them except for the fables that grip their blind belief.

And George Smith's adventures were now a fable that had to be believed.

Then Custer fell into a deep sleep. It was Suzy who woke him and brought him coffee. Now he did feel awful.

"Hi there, General," said Suzy. "How do you feel?"

"Could be better," Custer replied. "And you?"

"Fine, thanks."

"I saw the stars last night. And I think I may have walked on water."

"How was it?" Suzy asked.

"The end."

"The end of what?"

"The end. But I think it was beautiful, all the same. Sometimes you see things in a way you never have before. And that means you must be at death's door, even if you don't actually die. It's like looking beyond the door for a moment."

Custer was talking mostly to himself.

"Come on, General, a little more cheerful, please! What happened then?" Suzy asked.

"Nothing," Custer answered, "nothing at all."

He sipped the coffee slowly, pensively, as he looked straight ahead.

"Paper come yet?" he asked.

"I'll go see."

Suzy got up. She walked lightly to the door. When she opened it, Custer could see her naked body through the light fabric of her nightgown. He noticed the down on the small arch below her groin. Now at last that old longing came back.

END OF CHAPTER THIRTEEN

INTERMEZZO
AFTER CHAPTER THIRTEEN

Dear Abelard,

Are you happy now that I've let you have a look under Suzy's nightgown? I must confess that even after all these years I am still moved at the sight of those small details you glimpse in a fraction of a second when a beautiful woman wearing a nightgown has the light behind her. My wife and sister-in-law are in the habit of wearing very flimsy gowns in the morning when they are engaged in what are called housekeeping chores, and their apparel never fails to have an exciting and disturbing effect on my senses. The excitement is created by my wife, the disturbance by my sister-in-law. I may already have told you that I think it would be easy to overcome the guilt feelings I would surely have after any practical disturbance with my sister-in-law.

For years I have been singing the praises of Venice to

people from Milan, especially by extolling the human touch there is in Venice. When giving them an example, I used to contrast their cold supermarkets with the local Venetian fruit-and-vegetable man who was even willing to come to our house for just a head of lettuce. But I stopped the day I happened to discover that when my wife stands in our front doorway you can see her naked body against the light from the end of the hallway. No offense to the diligence of the fruit seller, but, as you know, my wife has always been considered a great beauty. News of the optical phenomenon must have reached our small neighborhood's shopkeepers rather quickly, because for quite some time they would rush over just to deliver a chunk of parmesan cheese. And very politely, I might add.

You are a hopeless materialist, and what attracts you in a woman is what might be called the total mass. You are not at all interested in the details, and yet the particulars are of fundamental importance. One woman may have a particular smile, another may have a bosom or thighs or maybe just ankles. I remember one woman, a singer-actress—and I'll even mention her name, Jane Birkin—whose eyes were, and still are, absolutely overwhelming. You may think I'm very corny when I tell you, but for a long time I dreamed about going around the world with her in a canoe. I could see myself sitting at the back rowing slowly and drawing strength from the look in her eyes as we toured the world's oceans and seas. But in my profession you must never attract a customer's attention for any but strictly professional reasons, so I was never able to put my plan into practice.

And it would have been a splendid opportunity to practice a sport that, together with my pale complexion, made me a hit with some of the girls, even though I had no special talents. But let's talk about the seductive power of languid looks or, if you prefer, languid eyes. The material part is easy; there's nothing hard about it: all you do is raise your lids a bit and look rather fixedly into space. What is hard is the spiritual part. Some people cannot manage to suggest that indefinable, deep sadness and achieve the slight tremor that hints at some intense emotion lurking just beneath the surface and trying to burst forth. You also have to convince the person you're with that the only alternative is to find the shortest route from the top of a skyscraper to the side- walk below. I was so good at it that when I practiced in front of the mirror, I would start to cry.

It isn't easy. You have to practice, but it helps to imagine losing a horse you loved or, in your case, losing a large amount of money. In any case, just let me say that I think that you can get a lot further just using your eyes than you can with a lot of talk. If you are a real artist, your lips will tremble only a brief moment before your left eye turns moist, as if it had just been hit with the lid of a pot.

Yours,

Arrigo

P.S. If you should ever publish these confidential letters of mine, I can imagine the reaction of onetime food critics (they are not big readers) who will have probably ended up as special correspondents in the world of psy- chometrics. They will rack their brain to figure out where this unexpected blow from a pot lid came from. I hope you let them give free rein to their imagination. But first offer them a couple of Bellinis in my name; that way they might understand how far blessed freedom can take you.

END OF THE INTERMEZZO
AFTER CHAPTER THIRTEEN

INTERMEZZO
BETWEEN CHAPTER
THIRTEEN AND CHAPTER X

Dear Abelard,

Now that we are coming to the end of my story—at least I hope so—I wonder if I might have left something out, some incident or detail that might perhaps illuminate your shameful but unaccountable ignorance.

The other day I was walking down a narrow *calle* in Venice, when I almost stumbled over Lorenza. You never met her, and even I could hardly remember her, because I hadn't seen her for more than thirty years. The first thing that struck me, however, was how perfectly preserved she was. The walls of the houses in the narrow alley reverberated, we hooted and howled so much. And we kissed and we hugged, and we tried in three minutes to exchange accounts of what had happened in three decades.

She was widowed twice, I never was; she married a third time, I haven't; she has one daughter, and I have one son and two daughters. So far so good. And we're both in marvelous health. I wanted to tell you about this meeting because of how Lorenza looked. Years ago no one would have believed she would live so long and look so wonderfully fit.

In those days she had just started studying English, and she wondered if she could take advantage of the fact that my father and I were going to England and come along with us, since it was her first time. In those days traveling was a serious business. You went to London by *Orient Express*—not the melancholy nostalgic imitation it is today; it was a real train that took you to faraway places that made poets say, "Leaving is a little like dying."

The time we went with Lorenza, my mother came to the station as usual with a white batiste handkerchief to wave us a last farewell as the train pulled out of the station and to wipe away her tears comfortably and discreetly. In those days a lot of emotion was expressed at train stations.

What I remember very clearly from that trip is the excitement of smoking a cigarette in front of my father for the first time. And with his permission.

We stayed the first few days in London at a small hotel owned by a woman who was totally deaf and had patronized Harry's Bar. There were two rooms on each floor and one bath on the landing. My father and I slept in one room, and Lorenza stayed in the other on the same floor.

With the excuse of going to the bathroom, I went to her room the evening we arrived. We had exchanged a couple of furtive glances on the train, and I got the impression Lorenza would not have been averse to some affectionate attention. There wasn't much time for preliminaries, because I didn't want my father to start wondering where I was and come to the logical conclusion. The first thing Lorenza said was that she felt very sad and lonely. I felt sorry for her, and it was mainly to console her that I put my arms around her. Perfectly normal. But I never expected what happened next.

The melancholy sighs ended almost at once, and Lorenza began sobbing. I didn't know what to say or do, and then suddenly our bodies were intertwined. I think it was because she was so sad. I tried even harder to console her, and I must confess that I forgot the boundaries between proper and improper conduct. At some point Lorenza's nightgown was off and she was all but shouting that I was killing her. Those were her exact words: "Help me, Arrigo, you're killing me!" And she said it over and over again.

Look, I'm an ordinary person and I have never had homicidal feelings toward anyone, but I was so intoxicated by the accusation that I did everything I could to make her keep on, and she shouted louder and louder, "Help, you're killing me!"

The upshot was that I was more dead than alive when I left her room. You might have expected Lorenza to die right after the last thrilling high note came from her gasping throat, but instead she recovered at once without a trace of loneliness or homesickness.

And that wasn't an isolated incident, because every night I left my room with the excuse that I had to go to the bathroom, and every night Lorenza and I played the same death scene. When I went back to bed the last night, my father put down the book he was pretending to read and looked at my face. He was worried because I looked so pale, and wondered if I had diarrhea, the only ailment that alarmed the family ever since an acute gastroenteritis almost sent me to my Maker when I was two years old.

Then I went to the famous manor house in Somerset, leaving Lorenza in London in full bloom. She even came up to see me a couple of weekends. Fortunately for me she stopped coming; otherwise, what with one thing and another, I am not sure I would ever have made it back to Italy.

It seems, dear Abelard, that women like that aren't as rare as you might think.

I doubt that you have ever met a woman like that. Otherwise, conceited as you are, you would have told me all about it. But if you ever do, I would advise you to run the other way. If you are ever at the pitch of excitement and someone screams "Help me, Abelard, you're killing me!" stop at once and let her die. Remember Lorenza! She takes flowers to the cemetery for two husbands, and her third husband was miraculously saved by running off with a flamenco dancer.

END OF THE INTERMEZZO
BETWEEN CHAPTER
THIRTEEN AND CHAPTER X

CHAPTER X

*The last three chapters are lettered X, Y, and Z. When
funding ran out, the scholars investigating the story of
Heloise and George had to abandon their research. Aside
from the facts given in these chapters, which are the
strict truth, what little else is known is fragmentary.*

George looked out of the airplane window and saw the
coast of Maine to his right. It was the first sight of land
after an endless sea of clouds. George could not remember a cloudless Atlantic crossing, and every time
he had happened to be on one of these airlifts, he
wondered if all that rain would pour out one day and
drown Europe. Before he knew Heloise, he had often
imagined himself as the skipper of an enormous ark
loaded with all kinds of animals. And usually the last
two human beings to embark were women, a blond
and a brunette. He would give them an austere
welcome-aboard that betrayed none of his cunning in
wanting them both on ship. Once the flood started, the
approaching end and his great charm would do the
rest.

Now he smiled at the thought of the imaginary
games he used to play for whole lazy days at a time. He
had never confessed them to his spiritual father,

though it did occur to him that he might be commiting a mortal sin. His religion showed the same severity toward thoughts, words, and actions. Essentially he agreed about actions, but he was less sure about words. And he never understood what thoughts had to do with it, so he saw no reason to be a stickler about them.

He noticed that Heloise was sleeping peacefully and decided not to wake her, though he would have liked her to see the coast. In another hour they would land in New York, the capital of the empire.

George had wonderful memories of the years he had lived there with his aunt from Alabama. It was clearer to him now that New York always made him feel as if he were in love. The city's rough edges and something very human in its asymmetry always evoked strong, deep feelings in him. His aunt had a small apartment on Sixty-third Street, between Fifth and Madison. He had never strayed far into the park, and rarely did he go farther east than Second Avenue or farther south than Forty-fifth Street. He was so fond of the neighborhood that he didn't need any place else, though he was fully aware of the many areas that made up the immensity he knew as Manhattan. Every time he went to New York, it was enough to breathe deep in the dry air. He was as happy strolling within the precincts of those four streets as he would have been walking along a friendly valley surrounded by high mountains.

Now he longed to share all this with Heloise. They would gaily run down the cracked pavements of Lexington Avenue hand in hand. The minute they let go, they would feel as anguished as if they were saying farewell at the edge of a desert, and they would be overwhelmed by the sight of the towering skyscrapers along Sixth Avenue. He wondered if she would be as awestruck as he by the Gothic steel pillars of the twin towers of the World Trade Center. They would laugh a lot, cozy and warm in the protective embrace of the city of man.

Then Heloise stirred. She opened her eyes and smiled. "When do we land?"

"Half an hour."

"I'm happy."

"So am I, and I love you."

"Me too."

She closed her eyes and seemed to go back to sleep.

END OF CHAPTER X

There is a gap at this point. The only thing certain is that George was awarded the Medal of Honor. This event is described in Chapter Y, and the end of the story is in Chapter Z. Our apologies to the reader.

INTERMEZZO
BETWEEN CHAPTER X
AND CHAPTER Y

Dear Abelard,

I am almost through with these letters, but I would like to try to explain what Heloise was really like. In addition to being essentially all aquiver, Heloise could probably be best described as a primordial woman. I don't know if you have ever had the good fortune to meet one.

I doubt it, because your suspicious nature, your repressed fantasies, and your insistence on always getting your money's worth would preclude the remotest possibility of ever meeting that kind of woman. But I have.

It was in America; I don't remember exactly when, I'm not sure if it was night or day, and I don't know if I was awake or dreaming. It was a period when I had nothing on my mind, and you know how sometimes an imperceptible detail can catch your attention—that's how I met a primordial woman. The first thing I noticed was her eyes. She was a brand-new American; she was actually born in Ireland. Her eyes were incredibly round, with the look of surprise that early man must have felt on this earth, and they were as blue as African oceans. Her ears were small, like those of the monkeys of the Serengeti Plain. Her high, full breast was divinely perfect, her hips were as round as the world, and her skin was white as the summer moon. I can't remember what excuse I made to introduce myself, but whatever remark I made, she said, "I know!" in a way I never heard before and will never hear again: drawling, warm, unhurried, and knowing, yet hopelessly and desolately final.

I swear, I never heard anyone say "I know" that way, and if you don't think that is a good enough reason to want to understand the source of such an unusual rendition of such an ordinary remark as "I know," it means that again you are very slow on the uptake. Sometimes I wonder why I take the time and trouble to write to you at all.

It would be a lie to say that I desired her at once. I just wanted to take a closer look and talk some more. I asked if she would have lunch or dinner with me, on the pretext that this would give us a chance to talk about her work. We made a date to meet at Smith & Wollensky's, a steakhouse that had something genuinely American about it. Naturally it was evening. She was very late, which I subsequently realized was an innate but charming defect. She was also a bit high, very cheerful, and not at all primordial. The whole staff of the restaurant frowned as we entered; they did not much approve of an older man taking a rather euphoric young woman out to dinner. I ordered everything I could to get the bill up to the impeccably respectable amount of four hundred dollars. I had to act the good paterfamilias when she spilled her glass on the pants of the man at the next table. And I all but fled from the restaurant ignominiously pursued by the hatcheck girl, who spurned the large, guilt-ridden tip and scornfully handed it back. I managed to hail a taxi all by myself, and Heloise—that was her name—sank back into the seat and gave me a full view of her round thighs.

I asked her up to my room when we got to the hotel, but her refusal, I later realized, was something inborn; it was one of the things that made her a primordial woman.

Let me explain—I wouldn't want you to think it was intense, lustful desire that had me in its grip that night. It was not like the time I went to Cortina with the set purpose of making love to a buxom lass from Bolzano while pretending I was actually looking for a temporary maid. I called her in Bolzano as soon as I got to Cortina to ask her why she wasn't there. She said she couldn't come because her father had just died, and the funeral was the next day.

I really don't know what possessed me, but the next thing I said was that I would come to Bolzano to be with her in her grief, and maybe we could meet, outside the café where she waitressed. She said she would look forward to my condolences about three in the afternoon, when she finished her shift.

And believe me, scared as you are of driving fast, you would never have survived the ride from Cortina to Bolzano, because the engine was sex-powered that day, and I took the curves on one wheel. I got stopped by the carabinieri outside Dobbiaco. They asked me where I was going in such a hurry, and I told them I was going to a friend's funeral. They let me go but suggested I slow down or there'd be two funerals instead of one.

I don't know if it was a reaction against grief or what, but the fact of the matter is that the moment we met we both decided at once to go to the nearest hotel we could find. We walked in, tossed our identification to the sleepy porter, and ran up to the room. I had the very exciting sight of her enormous butt all the way up the stairs. Once in the room, she reached greedily for the whiskey bottle, and from behind I tried to rip off her black silk apron. I saw that her black-seamed black stockings, which is what women wore before 1968, were held up by two garters on a thin elastic belt, also black, just over her lace panties. And that is where I directed the weapons at my disposal, i.e., my hands and everything else. She nearly shrieked with all the desire pent up in her body as she mourned with her mother and sisters her father's long illness and death. It was one of those incredible things—you don't know which way to turn and how many things you can do at once, and it hardly even seems possible until you have gone all the way and tried everything. And still there is always something unfinished, and there always seems to be something else you could try. There were other times I have been possessed by what might be called rampant desire, but the time with the girl from Bolzano was really the utmost. And I never saw her again.

As I was saying, I didn't have that kind of desire for Heloise, but her refusal stirred a different kind of desire, something deeper and more mature.

Cheer up now. I think the time has finally come to tell you what happened that first afternoon when

George and Heloise went upstairs at Harry's Bar in Beirut. I hope you're satisfied.

As soon as Harry closed the door after them, George and Heloise took off all their clothes. George kissed her slender, almost childlike, unworldly mouth. They rolled onto the bed, his lips brushed her suddenly stiff nipples, his chin caressed her full and welcoming abdomen, and then he sank his face between her legs. And as he did so, he was surprised by the scent. At first it was a sensation, a preliminary sign of distant sex. When he plunged into the lips of her vagina, he was enveloped by the soft and pungent, intense smell of earth rotting at dawn in the first rays of the sun, still not hot enough to assimilate the damp offal of nocturnal animals—an odor he didn't sense just with his nose: it went straight to his head, mentally repulsive yet instinctively attractive.

As a European, I would like to stop for this detail to show that America is also ahead of us in the matter of bidets. The reason the United States still doesn't import bidets certainly has nothing to do with trade protectionism. If they had bidets, a great many people would miss this wonderful gift of nature. I am speaking of odor. In Italy if you're lucky, the sexual organs smell of Palmolive soap, when they don't reek of some really inferior brand.

I could spend a whole month on the coast of Portugal sniffing the faint fragrance the trade winds waft from the distant coasts of America to our side of the Atlantic. This must be the reason so many explorers throughout history have risked death to sail west. Sailing upwind, to boot. Naturally!

Harry Cipriani, connoisseur that he was, never had

bidets installed in his rooms. How right he was, George thought. But let's get back to what I was telling you about, primordial woman.

Because it was the earthy sighs and cares that issued from her pleasure-sealed eyes (emanations George thought must be the food of the gods) that gave him courage. He plunged his tongue into soft warm channels and lingered over the tender firmness of her swollen clitoris. And then his mouth tasted the flavor of that odor. He had an irresistible longing to go deeper, farther down in pursuit of other unfamiliar rotundities, and he found them inexplicably yielding.

Meanwhile he swelled with pleasure almost to bursting, and there seemed to be tacit mutual agreement that the moment had come to climb back from those depths. His mouth was still full of these mysterious fragrances as it joined Heloise's in a deep kiss, while down below he approached the origin of life, which he could sense was ready and willing.

He entered slowly. He went all the way in and then came back for greater strength, as he went in and out and in and out. Small shouts of pain and joy issued rapidly from the throat of this primordial woman now totally obedient to the violent ongoing strokes of love. In the end, their powerful engines were humming together. The speed continued to increase madly, and the bushings melted, the valves broke, and all equilibrium was shattered in one ultimate, annihilating, definitive howl. Primordial woman. Heloise.

He sank exhausted in her embrace. When he looked her in the face, he could also detect the hint of a smile. He was calm again; his organ turned soft and rolled out of the friendly recesses. He turned slowly onto his side and sighed. He looked into her eyes, open now and full of wonderment. Now the corners of her mouth openly displayed a delicate conspiratorial smile. Heloise.

George would have liked to stop the sky. How could he stop the earth? Not even the room, nor the bed, nor his feelings could ever stop now.

"Heloise," George said.

"I know!" she replied.

That was the moment when the customers in the bar on the ground floor first heard the sounds and laughter of George and Heloise, and it went on that way for two weeks.

I know you would like to stop reading now that you have learned the things you were really interested in knowing. But since you have come this far, why not stick around to the end?

END OF THE INTERMEZZO
BETWEEN CHAPTER X
AND CHAPTER Y

CHAPTER Y

In which George is awarded the United States Army's highest medal.

The trees in the White House Rose Garden swayed lazily in the caressing breeze that came out of the west.

Two Marine battalions, drawn up stiffly at attention, stood facing each other in the open space in front of the President's residence. The Air Force Band, brasses glittering, stood behind. George stood at attention in dress uniform just behind the ranks of soldiers. A small crowd of elegant women accompanied by men in tails observed the proceedings from the garden only a short distance away.

Four plainclothesmen from the Secret Service came running from around the side of the building and fanned out. They were the President's advance guard. He made his appearance a moment later, wearing a light gray suit, and kept his eyes straight ahead. He walked quietly, but there was something remarkably youthful in his step. He stumbled at the edge of the walk but regained his balance immediately as one of the guards leapt forward to help him. The President smiled and made a wisecrack to the guard, who laughed heartily and winked at the crowd.

A gleeful laugh occasionally broke the silence. The President bounced up the three steps to the podium and stopped. He wore a very serious expression on his face. The band struck up the national anthem, and a rapid tremor of emotion ran through men and things alike. When the last note had vanished into the air, George stepped toward the President's platform. He went up the side steps, made a snappy about-face, and stopped a foot from the face of Reagan II. The two men greeted each other with an imperceptible nod. The Secretary of Defense handed the President an open red-leather case. The President removed the medal and draped it around George's neck. He put his hand on George's left shoulder and, continental style, brought his face to George's right cheek and then to his left. George thought he heard the President whisper something through his rather heavy breathing, but he couldn't have sworn to it afterward. It sounded like "son of a bitch." George wasn't altogether sure, partly because the President was giving him such a nice warm smile at the time.

George turned ninety degrees left and headed toward the steps. He stepped down slowly, pressing on the haft of his saber. When he was on the grass, he marched past the two rows of soldiers, who were presenting arms, and headed in the direction of the crowd.

END OF CHAPTER Y

We know only bits and pieces about the time George and Heloise spent in America. After a brief stay in New York, they spent more than a year with George's aunt in Alabama. We know that it was during this period that Heloise had a son. George and Heloise were not married, but George recognized his son. His aunt was able to die happy after seeing her great-nephew, and she was genuinely fond of Heloise. George inherited a substantial fortune and used a small part of it to pay his various debts to Harry Cipriani and his brothers. George and Heloise left their son in the care of George's old black nanny, and they left for Beirut. That was early October 2002.

INTERMEZZO
BETWEEN CHAPTER Y
AND CHAPTER Z

Dear Abelard,

I have just realized that I told you in a letter what
went on between Heloise and George in the room over
Harry's Bar in Beirut. And it's all your fault. That was
supposed to be part of the story, but nosy as you are, you
had to read it all by yourself. Knowing you, I imagine
you were totally absorbed by what are ultimately insig-
nificant details, and you surely failed to notice the one
important feature of that meeting—namely, the odor.

If I had to give up all but one of the five senses, I
think I wouldn't have a moment's hesitation. I would
keep my sense of smell. The odor of things. The intrinsic
essence projected into space. The extension of the invisible skein of reality. Memory's firmest image.

Our whole life and all our actions and reactions are
dictated by one single reality that leads us by the nose
back and forth, left and right: smell. We attribute a smell
to everything. Think how often we speak of the smell of
life or the smell of death—without thinking and, what's
more, without smelling.

But they really exist. The smell of life has a thousand forms. From the smell of fields, the smell of flowers, the smell of sea air, the magnificent fragance of springtime, the perfume of a sprig of mint subtly lurking in summer bushes. The aroma of mushrooms in the woods, pines against the sky, stones in wind-hewn rocks, clouds hovering low over gravel slides pouring down from the peaks to the crest of valleys, to the edge of the woods, where the wild smell of rhododendron waits to receive you before you sink in exhaustion onto the stony path and finally take in the odor of peaceful earth.

And there is the smell of death that comes into the house dressed in the clothes of old Anita, so tired, so desolate, and so desperately alone that the only thing she has left to leave behind is the smell of death. My poor old nanny, dearest Anita.

And there is the smell of church and holy water, incense burning on May evenings, and the ashes of joyful bonfires in August. There is the aroma of cornmeal churned and smoky in a huge copper kettle, and the smell of fresh hot milk blending with the pungent odor of damp manure in a summer barn. The smell of fresh-fallen rain on sunbaked countryside, the cold smell of night just before daybreak, the smell of my parents' bed, and the smell of our children at birth.

To keep all of this, I could give up sight and sound, speech and touch.

END OF THE INTERMEZZO
BETWEEN CHAPTER Y
AND CHAPTER Z

THE NEXT-TO-LAST INTERMEZZO

Dear Abelard,
Unlawful crap,
Lawful crap,
Awful crap,
I'm full of crap.
I wouldn't mind a peek
At the trilling little squeak
Of proper lady readers,
Put off by it,
Curious, excited a bit.
They'd like to know
Where does the crap go.
But,
NO SEX!
We're clean.
Death crap!
Dear ladies,
There it goes.

.

END OF THE NEXT-TO-LAST
INTERMEZZO

CHAPTER Z

Now they were back again on the same street, standing as they had at the end of those first two weeks, the first time they came out of Harry's Bar, when they idly strolled until they ran into Private Tom Margitai and he lent them his jeep.

They walked to the corner, and then for no apparent reason Heloise started running ahead of George. Perhaps it was her way of giving joyful expression to the happiness she felt. She quivered as usual on the high heels of her dusty black evening shoes. The way George watched her, he might have been a faithful Labrador staring after his master. George did not follow after, nor did he try to stop her. He felt drunk with happiness and with fatigue as well. He wished he could keep everything just the way it was at that moment—himself, Heloise, the dusty street, the blue of the sky and the green of the trees. He could have spent the rest of his life just looking at everything around him at that moment.

There was a sudden blinding flash of light to the east. For a brief instant everything around him, and Heloise ahead of him, turned as white as the glaring snow of a sunlit glacier. In a fraction of a second the blinding light seemed to annihilate all color just as surely as darkness would have. George did not complete this train of thought, because something caught his eye. It was a small white spider that had shriveled on a bright rock. It was just like the one he had seen one night on his bedroom ceiling. That was in 1988; he was a child then and was vacationing with his aunt in the country near Udine. It happened only a few seconds before the big earthquake.

This spider turned into a tiny ball vivid against the blinding surface of the rock. At that very instant Heloise turned round to smile at him. They silently looked into each other's eyes for an endless moment, as if an irresistible force held them apart. George could barely move his arms and legs. A violent hot wind sprang up, driven forward by a black cloud out of the east, the direction of the blinding light. A gigantic wall of sand swept the horizon, roaring like a thousand sea waves.

And the cloud brought fear in its wake.

"Heloise!" George shouted. He made a superhuman effort to reach her.

"George!" She moved toward him. She held out her hand, and George took it. The two of them were swept up from the ground by the fury of the incredible storm. The light was almost gone, and a terrifying darkness was swallowing all the colors of the world.

George held tightly to Heloise's hand as they whirled through the air. With an immense effort, he drew her near and wrapped his arms around her. He pressed his lips to her ear and shouted over the roaring wind: "I love you!"

She just had time to reply. "I love you!"

Then the heat melted everything. The bushes that swirled around them caught fire, and their torn clothing burst into flame, but they felt no pain whatsoever. And they were not afraid. Instead they felt an unexpected calm, a fortifying strength in their inmost parts, the bosom out of which we all are born. And that was their last sensation in this life.

THE END

CONCLUSION

The big cracker went off on the Beirut heights on October 10, 2002. In a matter of minutes, four hundred million people and sixty camels were dead.

For humankind it triggered the wise beginning of a long era of peace.

The camels probably could have done without it.

THE LAST INTERMEZZO

Dear Abelard,

So ends my manuscript, and if you are still with me, then, come what may, I know I have one reader at least.

In my last letter, I want to direct your attention to something that has never engaged your mind or your imagination. Death. I want to talk to you about death.

In the last couple of years before my father died, little things would come into his mind suggesting that the end was not far off. When we had breakfast together above Harry's Bar in Venice, he often seemed quite happy to discuss arrangements for his funeral.

"Listen, Arrigo," he would say, "I don't want any mass or priests when I die. All I want is a gondola with shiny brass fittings. I want a fir casket like poor people. That's how I want to be taken to the cemetery."

I would say, "All right, Dad." And I would also say, "There's plenty of time yet."

"Not that much," he would answer. He would forget

that we had probably had the same conversation just the day before. And we might repeat it even two or three times in the same week. He had used his brain so much all his life that he was fully aware of the fact that he was getting arteriosclerotic.

"My brain isn't working today," he would say, "but remember that if I say anything about Harry's Bar, I'm sure I won't be wrong about that."

And he was right too.

Two years later he had a terrible flu and sent for me. "Arrigo, it's not that I want to die, but I'm dying all the same. And nothing can be done about it." Then he asked me to get some olive oil and warm it up.

"Now oil me like my poor mother," he ordered. I rubbed the warm oil very slowly over his whole body. It was the first time I had ever seen my father naked, but it had no effect on me. I turned him first on one side and then on the other, until his whole body glistened with oil.

"Now I'm fine," he said.

It was another two months before he died. The funeral was just as he wanted it, except that there were seven gondolas instead of one, and four gondoliers rowed the one carrying his body.

I have had absolutely no warning signals, but I'd still like to take advantage of the end of this story to talk about my last wishes for the day I die. I might just as well start talking about it with you.

Well, my one great wish is to be remembered by the florists. What usually happens is that the deceased is not consulted and the family discourages floral displays by telling people "no flowers, but good works." This wretched little phrase is meant to foster good deeds that will eradicate those little stains that in the course of a lifetime inevitably will have soiled the pure soul of the dearly beloved and help him win plenary indulgence for all eternity.

Nothing could be further from the truth. A florist's curses are far more powerful than the distracted prayers uttered by the protégés of Saint Vincent de Paul.

So I categorically insist that the following words be printed in my death notice: "Lots of flowers and no good works"—and my death will be remembered for years as a red-letter day in the forsythia-and-gardenia trade. Don't worry about the salvation of my soul. In the years I spent in boarding school I accumulated thousands of prayers and enough indulgences to cover the sins I have already succeeded in committing, the sins I may yet manage to commit, and a great many more besides.

The spiritual exercises we did once a year at my priest-run school, for example, were always worth one plenary indulgence. Moreover, I did them at least three times. I followed all the rules—i.e., I didn't speak for three days, and I paid close and terrified attention to the preachings of a Jesuit who had been specially selected for his skill in describing the unspeakable torments of the eternal griddle. You heard things that would have made the toughest killer tremble in his boots. Solemn anathemas were rather wasted on us, because our sins hardly went further than coveting somebody else's girl-friend. Luckily for me, as I mentioned before, the memory of the blond hairs of Cousin Wanda's groin that time we were sailing at Torri del Benaco always outweighed the idea of taking out a soul-insurance policy with Lloyd's of Vatican City.

I do not remember who at the time told me how babies were made. All I remember is that one day a priest at school asked me if I knew. I said no, because I was afraid I'd have to do a penance. So he told me an incredible fairy tale that got off to a roaring start with bees and pollen. Afterward he asked me if I would like to enter the priesthood. All I could think of was what my father's reaction would have been, so I said that I would have to give the matter some thought. Then I decided to talk to my friend Jacky Ivancich; he's an ambassador now. I knew the priest had told him the story of the birds and the bees, and I thought it was time he learned the truth about how babies were conceived. I remember that he was quite hurt, chiefly by learning that the priest had been lying to him.

It is obvious that everything ever written about the afterlife, or rather the afterdeath, is pure fantasy. Take Dante, for example. There is nothing at all believable in his *Comedy*. There is no denying, however, that he didn't omit a single person, friend or enemy.

If you had to imagine a place that could contain all the men who, as their widows put it, have gone on to a better life, it would be difficult to conceive of a place where bodily sensations still survived.

The body dies at death; that's all there is to it.

So all that fire and ice and burning, and all those stories about the physical pain and joy of the life beyond, are certainly self-serving fibs.

Take a minute and think about the incredible "colossal" show that will be brewing up a few years from now in the Valley of Jehoshaphat. What with angel trumpets blasting and stern drums rolling, everyone who has ever lived will come in trembling submission to divine judgment.

It is quite obvious that whoever took down the words of the Prophet never owned a restaurant. If he had, his first concern would have been where to install the washrooms. Joel or whoever it was doesn't even mention the matter and leaves his reader in total darkness about a matter of the utmost importance. Think about it; billions of people in the same place, and the overwhelming majority of them probably have the runs, they're so frightened, but not one toilet. Joking aside, the story doesn't hold up.

I think you might imagine the only thing to survive would be a kind of collection of our individual thoughts and feelings, which would have a better chance of coagulating into some kind of whole depending on how deeply we were able to desire and feel things.

What I would like very much is a wide expanse in the heavens where all the good thoughts could come together, and another expanse, a little lower down and a little less heavenly, where all the bad thoughts could get together. Stop. This is my premise, and no one can disprove it—least of all you, materialist that you are; you've never given a thought to such things. It is my view, then, that George and Heloise, or rather their thoughts, quietly went off to that higher expanse. And they smiled, as it were, to see all those other thoughts that ever since the world began have helped men to be men and women women.

That came out all right too.

There are some other people I would like to see join the heroes of my story in the expanse that, for the sake of convenience, some people call heaven. I would like to see George and Heloise there together with General Custer, Suzy, Tom Margitai, and of course Harry Cipriani and all his family. Merchants no, because their life is too studded with temptations to get through it unharmed.

That way things wouldn't seem boring either, and one day—I hope it is still a long way off—I wouldn't mind joining all those nice people myself. I should also hope that the person in charge of the arrangements might work some inscrutable miracle and make sure they never run out of deliciously refreshing Bellinis for the enjoyment of all.